"Zoë, would you let me make love to you?"

His words turned the desire Zoë had already been feeling into a burning ache. Hadn't she wanted him to say those words, willed him to say them, since they'd first kissed?

"There's one thing you should understand," he said. "I'm almost certain that those men were after you because of me. In order to keep you safe, after tonight we can never see each other again. Knowing that, will you make love with me just this once?"

Just this once. The words played themselves over in her mind. Two days ago it had been only once with Jed Calhoun. Now it would be only once with Ethan Blair. But she wasn't going to say no. Tomorrow there'd be time enough to analyze why she might be attracting men who couldn't, or wouldn't, stick around. Tonight she was just going to indulge in her wild side again.

She smiled at him. "I thought you'd never ask."

Blaze™

Dear Reader,

When I first met Zoë McNamara and Jed Calhoun in
The Favor, I knew I had to give them their own book. Zoë
was *so* annoyed at her instant attraction to Jed. And Jed
had secrets, ones I was dying to find out. Add a forbidden
fantasy theme, and the possibilities were irresistible....

Even serious academic Zoë McNamara has sexual fantasies.
But her current goal is to get *one* particular man out of
them. The laid-back and incredibly sexy Jed Calhoun is
dominating her thoughts waking and sleeping, and he's
stirring up feelings Zoë hasn't acted on in a very long time.
Feelings that have always gotten her into trouble! But when
she decides to seduce him out of her system, it backfires.
Especially when she meets Ethan Blair—and feels the same
overwhelming chemistry with him...

I hope you enjoy Zoë's and Jed's *forbidden fantasy* as much as
I enjoyed writing it. (And if you read my RISKING IT ALL
Blaze miniseries, you'll run into some characters that you
already know.) For an excerpt and contest news, visit my
Web site, www.carasummers.com.

Happy reading,

Cara Summers

TWO HOT!
Cara Summers

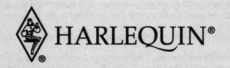

HARLEQUIN®

TORONTO • NEW YORK • LONDON
AMSTERDAM • PARIS • SYDNEY • HAMBURG
STOCKHOLM • ATHENS • TOKYO • MILAN • MADRID
PRAGUE • WARSAW • BUDAPEST • AUCKLAND

ISBN 0-373-79263-8

TWO HOT!

Copyright © 2006 by Carolyn Hanlon.

www.eHarlequin.com

Printed in U.S.A.

ABOUT THE AUTHOR

Since making her first sale, Cara Summers has written twenty-one books for Harlequin, Temptation, Duets and Blaze. Of the three lines, she feels Harlequin Blaze has challenged her the most. According to Cara, "It's the perfect line for a writer who has always been tempted by the *forbidden*." Her next book for the line will be a sexy Gothic. She has won several awards for her books, including the Golden Leaf, the Award of Excellence, a W.I.S.H and a Reviewer's Choice Award from *Romantic Times BOOKclub*. When Cara isn't writing, she teaches writing at Syracuse University and makes frequent trips to Florida to visit her two grandchildren—Marian, who is four, and Andrew, who is twenty months.

Books by Cara Summers

Don't miss any of our special offers. Write to us at the following address for information on our newest releases.

Harlequin Reader Service
U.S.: 3010 Walden Ave., P.O. Box 1325, Buffalo, NY 14269
Canadian: P.O. Box 609, Fort Erie, Ont. L2A 5X3

To Donna and Salvatore Buffa.
Thank you for all your support
(and for reading every book I've ever written!)
Most of all, thank you for being such good friends.
I love you both!

1

I WANT JED CALHOUN.

Zoë McNamara drew her bottom lip between her teeth and studied the words she'd just written on the first page of a fresh notebook. From the time she'd been a very young girl, she'd developed a habit of writing down her thoughts and feelings. Doing so had always helped her keep her focus and work through problems.

Jed Calhoun definitely qualified as a problem. She'd only known the man for two weeks, yet he could scramble her nerves with nothing more than one of those mocking looks of his. And when he touched her, even in the most casual way—the brush of his arm against hers as they entered a doorway—he sent her pulse rocketing.

Then there was the kiss.

Frowning, Zoë tapped her pen against the edge of the page. It hadn't been a kiss at all, not really, but it had stirred up desires she hadn't acted on in a very long time.

The problem was Jed Calhoun made her want to act on them. Ever since that "almost" kiss, he'd haunted her dreams, waking and sleeping. He was even beginning to interfere with her work. All she thought about was what it might have been like if he'd *really* kissed her.

Zoë badly wanted to pick up the notebook and throw it at the wall of her office. Better still, she wanted to go after Jed Calhoun and demand that he finish what he'd started. But she'd learned that giving in to what her parents referred to as the "wilder" side of her nature, especially with men, never solved a thing. She'd been there, done that her freshman year in college, and she'd learned her lesson. Hadn't she?

When the phone rang, Zoë jumped. A glance at the caller ID had her stomach knotting. It was her mother, no doubt wanting a progress report on her work.

Letting the call transfer to her voice mail, she rose and circled her desk, then began to pace the small Oriental rug. Lately, her parents had been pleased with her. She was a Ph.D. candidate in Psychology at Georgetown University. The current research she was doing with Dr. Sierra Gibbs on the dating and sexual practices of urban singles would be published, and that together with her degree would ensure her the kind of academic career that her parents felt was right for her.

Genetically, she was very suited to the kind of work she was doing with Sierra Gibbs. Her father, Dr. Michael McNamara, held a chair in theoretical physics at Harvard, and her mother, Dr. Miranda Phelps, was the dean of the engineering school at Stanford. But while raising her they hadn't been content to trust in genes.

They'd schooled her at home, providing her with private tutoring and special classes.

Stifling a little sigh, Zoë glanced around the small, meticulously neat office. This was the kind of world that her parents had raised her to fit into. And she was very good at what she was doing. So why did she feel so…trapped?

Moving to the window, she gazed out at the quad. The slant of the morning sun sent long shadows across the lush green grass. The two times she'd actually done what she'd wanted and strayed from her parents' expectations of her, she'd messed up. After her experiment with life on the wild side her freshman year in college, they'd insisted she go into therapy. They'd refused even to talk to her during the two months she'd worked at the CIA. Poor judgment and a sinful waste of her talents, they'd called it.

Taking the job at the CIA had been her last little rebellion against their plans for her. She'd thought that her work there would bring her the kind of adventure she'd always secretly dreamed about. She'd even studied karate in the hopes of eventually becoming a field agent.

But the only real excitement that she'd experienced in her work as a CIA data analyst had been of a vicarious nature, reading and analyzing the reports of one particular field agent whose code name was Lucifer.

Her job had been to analyze the probability that he'd carried out a hit on a fellow agent. Of course, he hadn't, but in the course of gathering intelligence on Lucifer, she'd become insatiably curious about the man.

His reputation was mythic. He was such a master of disguise that no one even knew what he looked like. His track record for getting the job done was flawless. There was even a theory that he didn't really exist, that Lucifer was merely a code name for a group of agents who performed dangerous and secret missions.

But Zoë didn't believe that. She'd read all of his reports, and there was something very distinctive about Lucifer's writing style, a kind of dry humor that appealed to her. And she admired the careful planning that was a hallmark of any mission he worked on. But the thing she'd admired most about Lucifer was the integrity that lay beneath all of his work. Lucifer was a man who could be trusted.

Was it any wonder that he'd become so firmly rooted in her imagination? He was living the life of adventure that she'd always secretly dreamed about. She'd even created a picture of him in her mind. He resembled his dark angel namesake—with longish dark hair and brilliant blue eyes. As she'd continued to gather and analyze information on him, Lucifer had begun to play a very active role in her fantasy life. She supposed that she'd even fallen a bit in love with him just as Shakespeare's Desdemona had fallen in love with the amazing stories that Othello had told her.

Zoë frowned. Desdemona clearly hadn't seen the real Othello. And her boss at the CIA, Hadley Richards, had told her that she hadn't "seen" the real Lucifer. He'd been very displeased with her final report on the superagent.

Zoë turned from the window to glance back at the notebook on her desk. Come to think of it, Jed Calhoun reminded her a bit of Lucifer. Not that he was a superspy. Her lips curved at the absurdity of that idea. But Jed did have a similar air of mystery about him. There had to be a reason why he was staying with his friend Ryder Kane, but not even her boss, Sierra, who was Ryder's fiancée, seemed to know the particulars. And Jed was living on the houseboat that Ryder kept on the Chesapeake Bay, not in Ryder's apartment in D.C. It was almost as if Jed Calhoun was in hiding. Why?

The sharp knock at her door had her jumping.

"Zoë, are you in there?"

Zoë recognized Sierra's voice immediately, but she'd barely turned around when Dr. Sierra Gibbs, her arms full of packages, breezed into the room. A month ago, Zoë mused, her boss would have asked permission before entering her office. But a lot of things had changed about Sierra since she'd met Ryder Kane, her new fiancé.

Before Ryder, Sierra and she had been mirror images of each other—once you subtracted the fact that Sierra was a tall blonde and Zoë was a short brunette. They'd both worn glasses, and they'd both worn their hair pulled back into a ponytail or a braid. They'd even worn the same kind of loose-fitting skirts and sweaters. During the time they'd worked together, she'd not only come to admire Sierra's work but she'd begun to look on her as a friend.

So she'd been happy to see how Sierra had blossomed since she'd met Ryder Kane. Her boss was currently dressed in a well-tailored suit in a shade Zoë would call pomegranate and high-heeled slingbacks that Zoë immediately envied. Sierra's hair fell in loose waves to her shoulders, and Zoë couldn't help admiring the style as her boss turned to glance at her.

It was only then that she saw that Sierra had pulled champagne, two glasses and a bag of imported chocolates out of the packages she'd been carrying.

"Sit down. We're celebrating," Sierra said.

"Celebrating what?"

Sierra paused in the midst of uncorking the champagne to stare at Zoë. "You're kidding, right?"

"No. What are we celebrating?" The way Sierra was looking at her made Zoë suddenly feel as if she'd been smeared on a slide.

"Merely the fact that your dissertation committee met this morning. Dr. Holloway just stopped by my office with the good news. Your proposed study has been approved. You're officially on the fast track to your degree. Did you forget that they were meeting?"

"Yes, I—" Zoë ran a hand through her hair. She'd completely forgotten. No doubt, that had been the reason for her mother's call, to make sure that her daughter hadn't fallen off the "fast track" again. "That's…wonderful."

Sierra's eyes narrowed as she handed Zoë a glass brimming with champagne. "You look like you need this, and not just for celebration purposes."

How could she have forgotten? Zoë wondered as she took a good gulp of the champagne and moved behind her desk to sit down. But she knew the answer. It was because she hadn't thought of anything but Jed Calhoun since that damn kiss that hadn't been a kiss at all.

Sierra tore open the bag of candy. "You'd better have some chocolate, too. Ryder gave me these, but on an occasion like this, I'm willing to share."

Zoë bit into a creamy chocolate truffle and tried to gather her thoughts. Sierra was going to grill her. She had that look on her face that she always got when she was interviewing one of the volunteers in their study. In a research situation, what Sierra went after, she usually got.

Sierra sat down and sipped champagne before she said, "Okay, spill it. What's wrong?"

Zoë stalled by taking another sip of champagne.

Sierra smiled at her. "I'm going to sit here until you tell me. Confession is good for the soul. That's what my sisters always tell me."

Sierra was the youngest of a trio of sisters. Natalie, the oldest, was a cop, and Rory, the middle sister, was a free-lance writer who'd been published in several major magazines. All three sisters had recently become engaged.

"Of course, I could try the same technique my sisters always use on me," Sierra said.

Zoë's eyes narrowed. "Does it involve torture?"

Sierra's eyes twinkled. "They haven't tortured me since I was little. Lately, they just tell me what they think is bothering me, and then launch right into lecture and advice mode."

Zoë began to relax. She and Sierra had never discussed Jed Calhoun. She'd never even mentioned his name. There was no way that she could know. "Go ahead. Give it a shot. Tell me what's bothering me."

"You're attracted to Jed Calhoun, and you're wondering if you should act on the attraction."

Zoë barely kept her mouth from dropping open. "How did you know?"

"Sweetie, the temperature in the room goes up by at least ten degrees whenever the two of you are together. Not to mention that the sparks shooting between you are so intense that the hairs on my arms stand up."

Zoë badly wanted to pace, but Sierra was now sitting in her pacing space. She was stuck behind her desk just as if she were in an interrogation room. After three beats of silence, she said, "I want him, but I don't want to want him."

Sierra smiled and nodded. "That's exactly how I felt about Ryder the first time I met him. I didn't know him then. I just knew how he made me feel, and I'd never felt that way before."

"Yes, that's it." Zoë gestured with her glass, then took another sip. "He has no right to make me feel this way."

"Men. They're all the same." Sierra topped off their glasses.

"He invades my personal space."

"Isn't that just like a man?"

"And he has no right to look the way he does," Zoë added.

"Absolutely not. He's as handsome as sin."

"Exactly." Even as she said the word, Zoë found herself picturing Jed in her mind—that long, lean body; the rangy, loose-limbed walk. The man never seemed to hurry. His hair was caught somewhere between sandy brown and blond, and he wore it long enough to pull back into a short ponytail at the nape of his neck. In the short time that she'd known him, he'd never worn anything but cutoff shorts or jeans and a T-shirt that molded each and every subtly defined muscle. Just thinking about him had the heat pooling in her center. "And his smile. I really hate it when he smiles at me."

"I hear you," Sierra said, then took another sip of her champagne.

"It's as if he knows things about me that he has no right to know."

"Unforgivable," Sierra said.

Zoë leaned forward. "You know there's more to him than meets the eye. On the surface, he seems so laid-back like some kind of California surfer who's living for the next perfect wave. But underneath, there's something else, a kind of power. It's hard to explain…" It was the same hint of power that she'd imagined in Lucifer, she realized. And she was attracted to that as much as she was to the easy, mocking charm. "If Jed Calhoun gets in your path, you won't get past him."

"Yes." Sierra nodded. "I noticed that, too."

Zoë took another sip of champagne. Maybe it was helping to talk about it. "He didn't even kiss me," Zoë said.

Sierra paused as she was reaching for the champagne bottle. "When didn't he kiss you?"

"The other night at the Blue Pepper when we were celebrating your engagement to Ryder. He invited me to dance and the next thing I knew we were behind one of those potted palms on the patio. He started to kiss me. And…" Zoë's voice trailed off as images flooded her mind, and her body began to heat. She could recall those minutes when she'd been in Jed's arms so clearly. Each sensation had been so intense.

There'd been a brick wall at her back and Jed Calhoun had been standing so close that she could see the sheen of dampness on the skin at his throat. Her own throat had gone dry as dust when he'd used two fingers to tilt up her chin so that she had to meet his eyes.

The tips of his fingers had been rough, and his touch had been confident and firm. This close, the flecks of green in those gray eyes had been darker, and for the first time, she'd detected no hint of the mocking laughter that she'd always seen there.

"I wish I knew why I want to kiss you so much." His voice had been rough, edged with a trace of annoyance.

The words had so clearly echoed what she was thinking that she'd wondered for a moment if he'd read her mind. While she was still thinking about that, he'd wrapped his other hand around the nape of her neck and lowered his mouth to within a breath of hers.

Her mind had emptied so quickly that she'd felt as if someone had pulled a plug. She'd known she should do something. Push him away. But he'd moved closer still until she'd felt the press of his body, firm, lean and strong against hers.

She'd risen on her toes to close the distance between them. Even then, his lips had barely brushed against hers. Still, the contact had sent a shock wave right down to her toes.

"More."

Zoë wasn't sure who'd spoken the word, but his mouth had moved against hers again. It wasn't really a kiss at all, and it was certainly not the kind of kiss that she'd expected from Jed Calhoun.

"You have a habit of biting down on your lower lip," he'd murmured. "Every time you do it, I want to do this." He'd drawn her bottom lip into his mouth and nipped it lightly. His breath had slipped between her parted lips and this time the shock wave had set off explosions. Every one of her senses had sharpened; each nerve in her body had snapped to life. She'd curled her fingers into his T-shirt.

"More."

His tongue had slipped between her lips and touched just the tip of hers, and she'd let out a shuddering breath she hadn't been aware she was holding.

Then as suddenly as it had begun, the kiss was over. Jed had lifted his mouth from hers and taken a step back. Her head had been spinning so that she hadn't even protested when he'd gripped her wrists and removed her hands from his shirt. At the abrupt loss of contact, her body had felt both icy and on fire, both weak and exhilarated. And deep inside of her she'd felt an overwhelming greed.

"Interesting," he'd murmured.

Interesting? She'd never experienced anything like it, and Jed Calhoun had thought the kiss was interesting.

"Earth to Zoë…"

Sierra's voice pulled Zoë abruptly back to the present.

"That must have been some kiss," Sierra said with a grin. "You said *more* twice while you were in that little trance."

Zoë frowned. "But he didn't give me more. I mean…" she broke off as pure anger bubbled to the surface of the emotions swirling through her. She pounded her fist on the desk and Sierra quickly rescued both glasses.

"If he were here right now, I'd make him finish what he started!"

"You go, girl!" Sierra said.

Zoë blinked. "But I can't. I won't. I—"

Sierra reached out and took her hand. "Why can't you, Zoë?"

"Because I have terrible judgment when it comes to men."

"Since when?" Sierra asked. "Seems to me you've got Jed Calhoun's number."

Zoë shook her head. "I see all men through rose-colored glasses. Take the guy I dated in college my freshman year. Bradley Harper. My therapist said he was my rebellion against my parents' plans for me. But I thought I was in love with him."

"What were your parents' plans?" Sierra asked.

Zoë waved a hand. "What we're celebrating right now—my upward climb to success in academia."

Sierra topped off their glasses again. "So what happened with Bradley Harper?"

"College was my first taste of freedom, my first chance to do things that I wanted to do. Bradley was my initial experiment with getting a sex life."

Sierra's eyes brightened with interest. "What exactly did you do?"

Zoë took another sip from her glass and leaned back in her chair. "I started with research. I looked like a nerd, acted like a nerd. You don't get much of a fashion sense when you don't get out much. So I collected information on sex from all kinds of places: scholarly journals, popular magazines. I observed other girls who were popular with men and I studied how they dressed, what kind of things they talked about. Finally, I did my best to change my appearance from nerd to sexpot."

"Amazing! I never would have had the courage to do that. If I'd never met Ryder, I would have stayed in nerd mode forever." Sierra passed Zoë another chocolate. "Did it work?"

"Yes." Zoë twisted the paper off the chocolate, but

she didn't taste it. "I picked out the boy I wanted to have sex with, and I didn't have to ask twice."

"You actually asked him?"

Zoë nodded. "It seemed the most efficient way. I'd watched other girls flirt, but I figured it might take a while to get the knack. Of course, I was a little surprised when he said yes. Bradley was incredibly good-looking and there were always girls around him. Lots of girls. That should have warned me."

Sierra poured more champagne. "What happened?"

Setting the chocolate aside, Zoë took a long swallow from her glass. She'd never told anyone the whole story, not even her therapist. "For a while everything was wonderful. The sex was great, so great that I suppose I fell a little in love with him. Then the semester ended, and he said he'd had a good time." Zoë glanced away for a moment and folded her hands in front of her. "He told me that he'd recommended me to a couple of his fraternity brothers and gave me their phone numbers."

"Did you call them?" Sierra asked carefully.

"Not right away." Zoë could feel heat rise in her face as she met Sierra's eyes again. "But I…missed the sex. And I wanted very much to be modern and cool. I thought that I'd been naive to think that Bradley and I would be a couple for very long. I went out with several of his fraternity brothers before I learned that I wasn't the first girl Bradley had passed along to them. It was something he did all the time. He even had a rating system for sex." She smiled without humor. "I'd gotten one of the highest ratings."

Sierra shrugged. "Well, I say good for you."

"You're not shocked?"

"I'm impressed by your gutsiness and disgusted with Bradley and his friends."

Zoë leaned forward a little. "Everyone in the frat house knew what I was like in bed. He'd described in detail things that we'd done together. I assumed the two young men I dated afterward had added to the data."

Sierra took her hand and squeezed it hard. "You were young and naive, and they were all pigs!"

Zoë felt a little band of pain around her heart ease. "Yes, they were. The next year when I came back to school, I had completely reverted to a nerd, and I buried myself in my studies."

Sierra studied her for a moment. "I can understand that. What's a bit harder to figure out is why you're still hiding from men and sex."

Zoë opened her mouth and then shut it. Sierra was right. That's exactly what she was doing, what she'd been doing for years.

"I did the same thing for a very long time. Until I met Ryder."

"Jed Calhoun is not Ryder."

"I'm betting he's not Bradley the jerk either."

"I don't know anything about Jed."

"He's Ryder's friend. They went to college together. You can tell a lot about a man from the kind of friends he makes and keeps. Plus, it wasn't too long ago that your research skills saved my life. If you want to know about Jed, I'll bet you could find out a lot."

"I don't know…"

Sierra squeezed the hand she'd been holding. "Now I'm going to give you some advice my sisters and I got from my father. Sometimes in life, you just have to take a risk."

2

ZOË SLAMMED DOWN on the brakes of her silver Miata and glared over the steering wheel at the water of the Chesapeake Bay. The directions Sierra had given her to Ryder Kane's houseboat had seemed simple enough, so why couldn't she find it?

The sun was glinting playfully off of the water, mocking her. Two days had passed since she and Sierra had talked and gotten a little buzzed on champagne, and she'd reached a decision about Jed Calhoun. She was going to give in to her wild side and have sex with him. But just one time. She had to do something to ease the yearning inside of her. It hadn't faded one little bit during the past two days. She just hadn't expected to have to act on her decision today.

The opportunity had presented itself when Sierra had called her two hours ago and asked her to bring the latest research notes out to Ryder Kane's houseboat and told her that Jed would be there.

Zoë pressed a hand to her stomach. If she'd had more notice, she might not be this nervous. And she might not be lost. This was the second time she'd taken a wrong turn and the second time the road had dead-ended at the water.

Was she subconsciously getting lost because she was having second thoughts?

No. Zoë gripped the steering wheel hard. She wasn't eighteen anymore, and she didn't have unrealistic expectations about sex or men. She hadn't made her decision in a fit of passion or rebellion or even while she was still affected by the champagne.

And she wasn't wearing rose-colored glasses. She'd run a check on Jed Calhoun, and he wasn't married. Her boss at the CIA had been, and she'd learned her lesson about steering clear of married men like Hadley Richards. If she'd just been a bit more worldly, she would have known that having business lunches with him and delivering reports to his hotel at night might give the appearance of their having an affair.

That was the reason Hadley Richards had given her when he'd asked for her resignation. Zoë felt the swift pang of regret that she always felt when she thought of having to leave her job at the CIA. She'd really liked the work, and up until she'd handed in her final report on Lucifer, Mr. Richards had been so enthusiastic about the jobs she'd done for him.

Even now, she wondered if she could have handled the situation differently. Of course, in private, Hadley Richards had apologized profusely. After all she'd only done what he'd asked her to do. He'd blamed the urgency for the work she'd been doing on Lucifer for his lapse in judgment. But he'd been firm about his request for her resignation.

Zoë dragged her thoughts back to her current problem. She was not that naive young woman anymore. And she'd discovered quite a bit about Jed Calhoun. He was rich, or at least his family was. His grandmother had founded a very successful cosmetics company which was still family owned, and it was currently being run by his parents and his sister. Jed hadn't gone into the family business. Instead, he'd elected to work for his government.

She hadn't been able to completely satisfy her curiosity about that aspect of his life because most of his files were classified. The one thing that had caught her attention was that he often used disguises, and that made her think of Lucifer again. Probably all CIA agents were skillful at using disguises.

She'd decided that it was good news that he worked for the government. He was probably in between jobs and he'd be gone before long. She'd also decided that since the chemistry between them was so strong— especially for her—it was highly likely that when they did make love, she could get him out of her system once and for all. Like a flash fire, what she was feeling would burn itself out and be gone.

She was banking on that, and there were plenty of narratives in the data she'd been collecting for Sierra that supported this theory. One round of hot, sweaty sex and she'd be free. One round and she could cross the man right out of her notebook. She could have her well-ordered life back.

She'd made a calm, well thought out, rational decision to have sex with Jed Calhoun, and she was not having second thoughts. Of course, if she'd had more time, she could have made the transition from nerd to sexpot a bit more fashionably. Instead, she'd barely had time after Sierra's call to change into a pair of new jeans and a tank top. The sexy underwear she'd intended to buy was still on her to-do list. The plain white cotton briefs in her bureau drawer were simply not appropriate, so she'd elected not to wear them.

Zoë drew in a deep breath and let it out. She was as ready as she could be to have sex with Jed Calhoun, so why then was she sitting here staring at the Chesapeake instead of propositioning Jed on Ryder Kane's houseboat?

Closing her eyes, Zoë rested her head against the steering wheel. Because she was afraid. What if he said no? What if he didn't feel the same way that she did? He'd pulled away from that kiss, hadn't he? When he'd walked away from her at the Blue Pepper, she'd had to lean against that wall for three full minutes before the feeling had come back into her legs.

Interesting is what he'd called that kiss. *Devastating* is what she'd called it. Zoë raised her head from the steering wheel and opened her eyes. Bottom line—she was afraid of what she'd always been afraid of—that she wouldn't, couldn't, live up to someone else's expectations.

Zoë lifted her chin. Well, Jed Calhoun might reject her. She was just going to have to risk it.

For the third time, she picked up the set of directions Sierra had dictated over the phone and studied them. She was going to find that houseboat. Wasn't the third time supposed to be the charm? And then one way or another, she was going to find a way to handle the Jed problem once and for all.

Shifting the car into reverse, she glanced in the rearview mirror and saw a dark SUV move through the crossroad twenty yards behind her. She might not have given it a second glance if it hadn't been for the fact that she'd seen it before—once on the main highway, and another time on the maze of roads that all seemed to inevitably dead-end at the water. So she wasn't the only one challenged by the dead-end roads in the area. Feeling somewhat cheered, she backed up, turned the car around and sped up the road.

THE BREEZE off the Chesapeake was cool and steady. Though it wasn't strong enough to move the hammock he was lying in, it still offered a pleasant contrast to the hot sun that managed to make its way through the leaves overhead. September was still hot in the D.C. area. But Jed Calhoun was growing tired of the lazy days of summer—tired of being trapped in limbo. And he was especially tired of being a "dead" man.

Two weeks of living on his friend Ryder's houseboat had allowed him to finish recovering from the injuries he'd sustained on his last mission, a contract job for the CIA that he'd very nearly not returned from.

Even now, he wasn't sure why he hadn't died six months ago in that alley in Bogotá. He'd suffered first a gunshot wound to the shoulder and then the leg. His last conscious thought as he'd faced the CIA agent who'd just shot him in the leg was that he was a goner.

Instead, he'd awakened in a small private hospital where the medical care had been surprisingly good. There was only one small problem. He'd discovered that Jed Calhoun was officially listed as dead, terminated by the agent who'd shot him in the leg. The real kicker was that the orders to take him out had come from the director of the CIA because he, Jed Calhoun, had killed Frank Medici, a career operative with the CIA who'd penetrated a large drug cartel in Colombia.

It was a lie. But he'd been in a bar with Frank and delivered a message to him moments before a bomb had destroyed the entire building.

During the past two weeks, Ryder had called in a few favors from his contacts at CIA headquarters and learned that Jed's motive for killing Frank Medici had been money. Supposedly someone in the Vidal drug cartel had learned of Frank's true identity and hired Jed to take him out. Right now there was a million in American dollars in an offshore account in Jed's name.

The frame was neat and conclusive. He'd been in that bar. He could have planted that bomb. And the money trail led to him. As long as Jed Calhoun remained "dead," the case was closed. And until Ryder and he could prove that Jed hadn't killed Frank Medici, he couldn't rise from the dead.

He was trapped in limbo all right. The one thing he did know was who'd shot him and left him in that alley. Agent Bailey Montgomery, who was currently one of the best data analysts at the CIA. They'd sent a desk jockey to terminate him. That part grated a little, but it had been clever of them to send a woman. It had made him less suspicious when she'd suggested an alley for their meeting. He'd slipped up there, but so had she. He was still alive.

But it wasn't just his own frustration that was grating on him. He also had a feeling deep in his gut that his time was running out. A week ago he'd helped Ryder out with a case involving Ryder's fiancé, Sierra Gibbs, and he'd had to appear briefly at a major D.C. party. A lot of the capital's movers and shakers had been there, including Bailey Montgomery. She might have spotted him. A nagging little hunch told him that she had, and if she had, he had no doubt she'd come after him.

What he needed was just a little something to go on. All it would take was a thread that he could pull on until the whole fabric unraveled. Since Ryder had finished the case involving Sierra, his friend had been working 24/7 to come up with something, but so far Ryder had been drawing blanks.

A short burst of laughter—Sierra's and Ryder's— carried clearly to him despite that the hammock was a good three hundred yards from the houseboat and blocked from view by some trees. Jed's frustration increased.

In the short time that Dr. Sierra Gibbs and Ryder Kane had been together, Jed had found himself envying Ryder. It had been a long time since he'd allowed himself to have a serious relationship with a woman. Doing freelance contract work for various government agencies was not conducive to having a stable love life.

Which was another reason why he was determined to get his life back. Restlessly, Jed shifted again in the hammock.

Another burst of laughter floated to him on the breeze. He missed that sharing of jokes, the after-sex conversations—and hell, he might as well be honest. He missed the sex, too. No doubt that was why he found himself spinning erotic fantasies about Sierra's mousy little research assistant, Zoë McNamara.

From the time that he'd first laid eyes on her, he hadn't been able to shake her loose from his mind. At first he'd found that curious because she wasn't his type. Usually he was drawn to tall, leggy blondes.

Zoë McNamara was the total opposite of that. In terms of appearance, the most he could give her was *cute.* She was short, barely an inch or so above five feet tall, she had glossy, dark brown hair that she wore pulled back in a ponytail or a braid. He'd never seen her legs because she usually hid them under long skirts. She hid her eyes, too, behind oversize black-framed glasses. Maybe that was why so many of his dreams were fueled by the challenge of getting her out of those ugly clothes and out from behind those nerdy specs.

She was a prickly little thing, too—didn't like her personal space invaded. Naturally, it had amused him to invade it at every opportunity. But each time he got close to her, he had an urge to get closer still.

A couple of nights ago at Ryder and Sierra's engagement party, he'd asked her to dance. And he'd kissed her. Or at least that had been his intention when he'd drawn her behind that cluster of potted palms on the patio of the Blue Pepper.

But he hadn't kissed her, not fully, not the way he wanted to kiss her. Something had made him step away at the last moment. That wasn't like him. Jed frowned as he thought about it. The last woman who'd made him hesitate like that was Molly Jo Beckworth in third grade. Jed smiled at the memory. Molly Jo had been tall, blond and beautiful, and on his second attempt to kiss her he hadn't been hesitant at all.

But Zoë McNamara wasn't his first love—or any kind of love at all. She was a woman who had attracted him on first sight. Sometimes the chemistry worked that way. In Zoë's case, the magnetic pull between them had increased each and every time he was anywhere near her. He should have ignored it. Ignored her. He had no business making a move on a woman, any woman, until he got his life back. But he couldn't seem to resist her. Kissing her had probably been inevitable. And it had shaken him to the core.

In his mind, Jed let himself drift back to the moment. She'd certainly been willing. The moment he'd brushed his mouth over hers, her lips had parted in a welcoming invitation. When she'd risen on her toes to close the distance between them, he'd taken his first sample of her taste.

Oh, she'd been so much sweeter than he'd expected. Even sweeter than the sugar cookies he used to swipe from his mom as fast as she could make them. He'd barely absorbed her flavor when her breath had shuddered out, and the sound of her surrender had nearly sliced right through his control. Then, in the next instant, her hands had gripped his T-shirt and she'd demanded, "More."

It was that sudden irrefutable proof of the bright passion that lay beneath the surface of Zoë McNamara, struggling to be free, that nearly shattered him.

Oh, how he'd wanted to forget where they were and touch her. He'd wanted her out of that oversize man's shirt and that skirt. He'd wanted to strip away the practical underwear he knew was underneath.

The desire to use his hands on her, to let his fingers and palms explore her skin, molding every inch of her, had become a knife-sharp ache.

An image had filled his mind of taking her right where they stood. The music was loud enough, the palms thick enough to conceal them. He'd pictured it so clearly in his mind—her legs wrapped around him, her back pressed against the brick wall as he took that first hot, wet slide into her. It would have been wild, reckless, and wonderful. He was skilled enough and she'd been ready.

He still wasn't sure what had given him the strength to pull back. He suspected that it had something to do with his carefully honed survival instinct, and he wasn't sure he was comfortable with that explanation.

What he was sure of was that when he'd learned she was coming today to deliver some research to Sierra, he'd stuffed a couple of condoms in his shorts pocket. In case he got lucky? Or in case this time he wouldn't be able to control himself? Either way, that one small action of making sure they would have protection clearly revealed just how much of a pull the woman had on him.

In the days since that kiss, he'd done some research on her. She was the daughter of two very highly acclaimed professors, and from what he'd gathered, she'd been a sort of joint project of theirs, a highly intelligent child that they'd pushed and prodded, supervising every aspect of her education. Each of them had published articles about her.

He thought of his own happily married parents and his kid sister, and all the fun they'd had growing up. He suspected that in comparison, Zoë had had a very lonely childhood as well as a highly pressured one.

Her academic credentials were certainly impressive, and Sierra raved about her work. It was the two months she'd spent as a data analyst at the CIA that had surprised him. She'd resigned shortly before he'd been "terminated," and her short tenure there had given him his first clue that the real Zoë McNamara might be a sharp right turn from the academic nerd she so carefully projected to the people around her.

The kiss they'd shared certainly provided evidence of that. Maybe it was the contrast that fascinated him so.

With a sigh, Jed shifted again in the hammock. He shouldn't be thinking of Zoë McNamara. He shouldn't be thinking of the fact that she'd be here in a short time. Or of the fact that he had condoms in his pocket. Nevertheless, his lips curved in a grin. In the past few days, he'd created some very interesting fantasies about Sierra's little assistant, some of them in this very hammock. Sex in a hammock called for invention and ingenuity, but it was invariably worth it.

A muffled crash came from the houseboat. Lifting his baseball cap, Jed flicked a glance in that direction. Speaking of sex…

Jed sighed again. He really had to get on with his life. He was growing tired of feeling like a third wheel now that his host and old friend had forged a solid relationship with Sierra Gibbs. She was spending more and more time on the houseboat, and he tried to give them privacy. In deference to his presence, they retired pretty frequently to Ryder's cabin, but it was clear he was restricting their freedom of sexual expression.

He had to do something and soon. It wasn't just boredom or restlessness motivating him. It was also that slim possibility that Bailey Montgomery, his would-be assassin, had spotted him at that party.

And there'd been something else that had occurred on the night he'd kissed Zoë. After the party, he and Ryder and Sierra had driven her home, and he was pretty sure that they'd been followed by a dark-colored car—a van or an SUV. It hadn't gotten close enough for him to be sure. He'd been driving Ryder's car, and it hadn't taken much to lose the tail. He'd delayed telling Ryder this weekend because Sierra was here, but he was going to have to tell him soon.

Maybe his best strategy was to make the first move. What did he have to lose if Bailey Montgomery already knew he was alive?

Jed pulled his baseball cap down over his eyes to block out the sun. It was a big *if,* but certainly worth considering. In the meantime, he was going to take a nap. In some of the toughest situations he'd found himself in, he'd always relied on his subconscious mind to come up with a plan.

He hoped it wouldn't fail him now.

3

ZOË BRAKED HER MIATA to a stop, then peered at Sierra's directions. Ahead of her was a houseboat, white with green shutters just as Sierra had described it. To the right was Ryder Kane's sporty red convertible. Sufficiently reassured that she'd finally arrived at her destination, she climbed out of the car, lifted the box of note cards from behind the driver's seat and walked toward the boat.

Nerves knotted in her stomach, but she made herself put one foot in front of the other. The time for analysis was over. She was going to act. She should feel relieved instead of feeling like Joan of Arc climbing up her funeral pyre.

She was ten feet away from the houseboat when she heard a muffled moan. Dropping the box, she raced forward, but when she heard the second moan, louder this time, she stopped short. The third moan was longer and accompanied by a rapping sound as if something was bumping against the wall in a steady rhythm. Zoë was pretty sure that no one was in trouble or pain. Chances were good that Sierra and Ryder were making love.

And she'd been about to break in on them. Not her best move under the circumstances. As the rhythm of the rapping noise increased and she realized that she was just standing there eavesdropping, she turned and hurried back to the box she'd dropped.

Dropping to her knees, she began to gather up the note cards that had fallen out of the box. But in one part of her mind, she was picturing what Ryder and Sierra were doing, and the images triggered a hot lick of lust inside of her.

Pushing the mental pictures away, she focused on the note cards. Sierra used blue ones and hers were white. Methodically she began sorting them into two piles. But the images slipped back into her mind—only this time, it wasn't Ryder and Sierra that she saw. It was Jed Calhoun and herself, limbs entwined, bodies locked and moving in that quickly escalating rhythm that she was listening to. Heat flooded through her with such intensity that for a moment, she thought she just might melt into a pool on the ground. So vivid were the pictures in her mind that she could almost feel Jed's long, hard body pressing against hers, and she could imagine quite vividly what it would feel like to have him pushing into her, withdrawing and pushing in again. She wanted, oh, she wanted…

There was another sound, a long feminine cry, and there was no mistaking the satisfaction in it. Then there was silence. Zoë pressed a hand against her stomach. Her insides were so hot, so empty, and longing for…something. When was the last time she'd achieved that kind of release? That kind of pleasure? Years ago.

She should leave. She should get back into her car and drive around a bit. After bunching all the note cards together, she stuffed them back into the box.

And then suddenly, she felt him. It wasn't a sound that warned her. It was her body's reaction that told her Jed Calhoun was there even before she turned and saw him standing at the edge of the trees, wearing nothing but cutoff shorts and a baseball cap.

Her mouth went dry as dust, and a rush of sensations cartwheeled through her. Heat. Cold. An electric shock of lust. She couldn't move. She couldn't even think.

He was watching her in that intent way he had. Even at this distance, she could feel his eyes moving over her, the heat of his gaze on her skin. The sensation was as real as if he were touching her.

She wanted him to touch her. She wanted his hands on her. More than that, she wanted her hands on him. But he wasn't moving. He was a man who could wait for what he wanted.

Lifting her chin, she rose to her feet. Well, she wasn't going to wait for what she wanted.

JED HADN'T THOUGHT it was possible for his body to get any harder, but it did with the first step she took toward him. He'd been watching her for some time, and the sounds coming from the houseboat had made his head spin with images of what it would be like to touch her until she was hot and wet and slick, to thrust inside of her and feel her close around him….

If he'd gone to her now, he wasn't sure he could have kept himself from taking her right here on the spot. Control was something he'd always prided himself on. But it seemed to disappear around Zoë. Case in point, he hadn't been able to stop himself from getting out of the hammock and coming to see her. Now he was willing her to come to him.

That's what she'd done in the little daydream he'd been having in the hammock before he'd heard her car. The woman he'd conjured up in his mind had risen out of the water like a nymph or some kind of sea sprite, and she'd walked toward him just as she was doing now. Her hair had been loose, just as it was now.

The punch of desire that hit him low and hard was new and very real. So was the sharp need to bury his hands in that hair.

In the daydream, she'd been out of those baggy, drab clothes of hers. He'd imagined her in a bikini, but in the snug jeans and tank top, she looked even sexier. That slender, compact body was more appealing, and those legs were much longer than he'd imagined.

How often in life was reality better than a fantasy?

She didn't stop until she was nearly toe-to-toe with him. Though amber-colored sunglasses covered her eyes, he felt it like another little punch in the gut the minute her gaze locked on his.

She cleared her throat. "Would you like to have sex with me?"

Jed felt his mind begin to empty, and he was pretty sure his mouth had dropped open. Talk about fantasies. But this was real, right? He badly wanted to pinch himself to make sure, but he didn't think he could move his hands. He concentrated on finding his voice.

She certainly wasn't having any trouble using hers. He could see her lips moving, and through the buzzing sound in his head, some of the words were getting through.

"I'm not crazy—don't think I am—it's just that you keep slipping into my thoughts and my dreams."

He could understand that and even sympathize with the annoyance he heard in her voice. That was real. And so was her scent: sunshine and something that reminded him again of homemade sugar cookies. He wasn't sure how long he could wait to take a bite of her.

"So…what I'm thinking is we have sex—if you think that you'd be open to that?"

Open? He felt another punch of desire and struggled to focus.

"I'm not suggesting anything long-term. Just a brief liaison."

"Liaison." Relief streamed through him that he'd not only found his voice, but he'd managed to get his tongue around the word.

She waved a hand. "I just need to get you out of my system so that I can think again."

"I'm in your system?" That was good to know, since

she was definitely in his. Some of the blood seemed to have returned to his brain because he was thinking again, and he was pretty sure he could move.

Nodding, she drew a deep breath, then hurried on. "I know that you may not be as attracted to me as I am to you, but maybe there's something that I could do. Some particular fantasy that you're into. I'd be willing to experiment a—"

"Hold up." He was tempted to let her go on, just to hear what she'd say, but he was even more tempted to see her eyes. He reached over and pulled off the sunglasses. Her eyes were almond shaped, like a cat's eye. Funny that he'd never noticed that when she'd worn the owl glasses. And this close, they were the color of rich, dark chocolate flecked with gold.

"Why did you do that?" Zoë asked.

"I was curious about what you would look like without glasses," he said. "In reality. In my fantasies, you're always underneath me and I'm inside of you when I take them off of you."

"Oh."

He had the satisfaction of seeing her eyes darken and cloud.

She blinked. "Well…then, I suppose…" She blinked again. "Are you saying that you'll have sex with me?"

She was so damn cute. He had to touch her then, drawing one finger along her jawline as he'd done so often in his fantasies. Her skin was even softer than he'd imagined. "You had me at 'Would you like to have sex with me?' Since then, I've been fighting off the impulse to drag you to the ground and take you right here."

She blinked again and glanced back at the house-boat. "That's probably not a good idea. We could be interrupted."

"Good point." Taking her hand, he drew her into the trees.

ZOË SWALLOWED hard as she walked with Jed. She was going to have sex with Jed Calhoun. In a minute, *he* would sink in. To her. In a minute, they'd actually do it. When he'd touched her, just that gentle stroke of his finger along her jaw, heat had arrowed through her, and her toes had curled. No man had ever made her toes curl before.

So why was there a little knot of panic forming in her stomach? She stopped short, and he glanced down at her.

"Having second thoughts?" he asked.

"No." She looked up and met his eyes. He suddenly seemed taller. Sunlight was filtered through the leaves overhead, and in the shifting shadows, Jed Calhoun looked more dangerous, too. For some reason, that made her want him even more. The thought occurred to her that she might just be getting in a little over her head.

"What then?" he asked.

She moistened lips that had gone dry and searched for something to say. "Protection." She tugged her hand away. "I have some condoms in the car."

Before she could even turn, he had her hand again.

"I've got it covered." With his free hand, he patted his pocket. "And that's not the only thing that's got you hesitating. We don't have to do this."

"Yes, we do." She met his eyes then. "I don't think I could stand it if we don't. It's just nerves. I haven't done this in a while."

"Good."

She watched in fascination as his lips softened and curved. Something inside of her eased.

"That means we're in the same boat, because I haven't done this in a while, either," he said as he drew her farther into the woods. "But you know what they say? It's like riding a bike. I'm banking on the fact that it will come back to me."

They'd reached a small clearing where a hammock swung between two trees. It was so quiet that she could hear leaves rustling overhead.

"I never learned how to ride a bike," she confessed as nerves fluttered again in her stomach. There'd been too many classes, all that extra math and science that her parents had insisted she take so that she could live up to their expectations.

Jed squeezed her hand. "Not to worry. From the time I was about seven, bikes were my passion. I had dreams of racing in the Tour de France."

She met his eyes. But he didn't say any more. He seemed to be waiting for her to make the first move. She moistened her lips and cleared her throat. "I did offer you a fantasy. Just how kinky do you like them?"

He was studying her now, and she could feel the heat rising in her cheeks. What was he seeing?

But she knew the answer to that. He was seeing a plain-looking woman. She didn't kid herself that in the short amount of time after Sierra's phone call she'd had time to transform herself.

Suddenly, he wiggled his eyebrows at her. "On a scale of one to ten, ten being very kinky, I'd say I like my fantasies at about a twelve." Then he shot her a quick grin. "Just kidding. Why don't we try this?" Leaning down, he gripped her chin and brushed a quick kiss over her mouth.

A dozen little explosions of pleasure shot through her. His lips couldn't have been touching hers for more than an instant, yet every single atom in her body seemed to be reaching out to him, and a delicious weakness had attacked her limbs. If he hadn't been holding her up by her chin, she just might have sagged to the ground.

"Truthfully, on the kinky scale, I'm pretty flexible," he continued. "How about you? You did say that you'd be willing to experiment a bit. Did you mean it?"

When she moistened her lips this time, she tasted him—something dark and male and delicious. She thought that with Jed she just might be able to get to a twelve herself. "Sure."

"Good. Because I've been having these recurring fantasies about making love to you in this hammock."

Zoë shot the hammock a quick look. Then she

checked out the two trees. They looked pretty sturdy. Still… "What if we fall out?"

"We won't. I've explored the possibilities pretty thoroughly in my mind, and I have a plan."

"Oh." Zoë drew in a deep breath. "Okay."

"Great," Jed said. "But first, we have to strip."

4

"Strip?" Zoë swallowed hard.

Jed unsnapped his shorts. "Yeah. It'll be challenging to get our clothes off once we get in the hammock. It's pretty close quarters."

Her gaze froze on his zipper as he lowered it. Then his cutoffs slid to the ground. He wore only the thinnest pair of black briefs. For a moment, she simply stared. If she'd had any doubt at all that he was enthused about her proposition, it was put to rest.

"Need some help?" he asked.

"No." She wasn't going to think about her body. *Just do it.* She had a wild side. All she had to do was tap into it. Gripping the edges of her tank top, she pulled it over her head and dropped it on the ground. Then she ordered her hands to unsnap her jeans, pull the zipper. Somehow, she managed to wiggle out of the jeans.

"You don't wear underpants."

The hoarseness in his voice had her eyes flying to his. "Yes, I do. Usually." She just hadn't been able to put on the sensible cotton briefs she usually wore, and… "I didn't have time to buy anything sexy."

He smiled at her in that slow way he had. "My good luck. One of my favorite recurring fantasies is about a girl who never wears underpants."

She stared at him. "That's…so adolescent."

He laughed then, the rich sound filling the air, and Zoë felt some of her tension ease.

He took one of her hands. "Are you telling me that you don't fantasize about guys who don't wear undershorts?"

She bit back a smile. "Not yet. And you're still wearing yours."

"I want you to pull them off."

"Another fantasy?"

He winked at her. "You've got my number."

She reached out and slipped her fingers beneath the elastic waistband, then slowly tugged the briefs down until they slid to his feet. She caught herself staring again. "I think I have a fantasy now," she said.

"Good."

Before she was quite aware of what he was doing, he'd reached behind her and unfastened her bra. She felt a whisper of cotton on her skin as it slid to the ground.

"Lovely." With one finger he traced a path along the slope of each breast.

"I'm small," she said.

"You're neat," he corrected.

He slipped his hand into hers again and drew her closer. "Before we get to the kinky part, I want to kiss you." He tipped her chin up as he lowered his head. "I've been thinking about kissing you for a long time."

His mouth was so close that she could feel his breath on her lips. "Me, too."

"Nice to know that we're on the same page," he murmured as he framed her face with his hands and urged her up onto her toes. Even then, he only pressed his mouth lightly against hers before he withdrew. But he followed with another kiss, lingering longer before he broke it. "I've been wondering about the fit."

As far as she could tell, the fit was very good. Each new angle that he tried seemed to get better. And his taste—the wonderful male flavor was as good as choc- olate. When his tongue finally touched hers, she had to reach out and grab his waist to steady herself. This time when he drew away, she slid her hands up and grabbed his shoulders to pull him closer. "More."

"Yes." Finally, he deepened the kiss. But he was still gentle, still tasting her as if he had all the time in the world and intended to take it. Pleasure streamed through her with an intensity that she'd never felt before. She could smell the heat of the day, the earthy scent of the trees and ground, and the sea. But she could also smell Jed—a mixture of soap and sun and man. She was so aware of that firm yet gentle mouth and the warmth and strength of the hands that framed her face—she felt the pressure of each finger. She was melting, floating, and he wasn't even touching her. Not really. When he nipped her bottom lip with his teeth, the sharp stab of desire took her by surprise. She pushed against him.

When he drew back, she said, "I think it's time to get into the hammock."

He drew a thumb over her bottom lip. "Not yet."

She pressed her hands more firmly against his chest. "Why not?"

"Once we get in there, foreplay becomes problematic. Besides, I've never been a fan of the wham-bam-thank-you-ma'am kind of sex. I want you ready."

"I am." For heaven's sake, she was pretty sure she'd been ready the first time she'd seen him.

He moved his mouth to her earlobe and gave it a quick nip. "Maybe I'm not. I've wanted to be inside you since the first time I saw you. I want you wet and slick."

The whispered words, the warmth of his breath, had a tremor moving through her. She managed to take in enough air to say, "I'm practically melting."

His gaze returned to hers, and he smiled that slow, easy grin. She was very much aware that his mouth was only a breath away from hers.

"Are you always in such a big hurry?" he asked.

Heat rose in her cheeks. She'd never thought about it before. "I guess." But perhaps her sexual experience had been limited to men who'd always been in a hurry.

"Sugar, anticipation is half the fun. But in the interests of compromise, I think we can proceed to step two."

Before she could react or even think, he spanned her waist with his hands, lifted her and carried her toward the hammock. Then, to her surprise, she found herself on her feet again with her back against one of the trees.

"Why don't we step up the pace just a bit?" His mouth covered hers again, and this time he probed more deeply with his tongue. His hands weren't quite gentle as he moved them up her sides and then slid them to cover her breasts. The heat that shot through her was even more intense than what she'd felt before. Her toes curled into the cool grass.

But still he moved slowly as if he had all the time in the world—as if he wanted as much time as he could get. Sensations streamed through her in a series of contrasts: the coolness of the breeze off the water and the furnacelike heat radiating from his body; the strength of those hands stroking down her arms, up her sides, yet the restraint in the patient, thorough exploration of her skin; the hammering race of his heart against the palms of her hands and the slow, gentle movement of his thumbs over her nipples. She felt as if she were sinking and floating at the same time.

When he lifted his mouth from hers, she whispered, "Please." But she wasn't sure if she was pleading with him to stop or to go on. And on.

His mouth was poised above hers. "Have I convinced you yet of the benefits of foreplay?"

He was teasing her. Again. She lifted her chin and met his eyes. "Maybe."

"I guess I'll just have to try harder," he said. "You're a research scientist, right?"

"Yes."

"Then you probably run experiments all the time."

Her brows drew together. "No. I mostly gather and analyze data."

"That'll work. I'm just going to gather a little data on what you like. We'll start with this." Leaning down, he ran a string of nibbling kisses along her shoulder until he reached her throat. Then he nipped at the ligament just where her shoulder joined her neck. She felt her body go limp as a sharp streak of pleasure shot through her.

"Better?" he asked.

"Mmm." Even her lips had grown weak. She couldn't seem to form a coherent word.

His chuckle was a rumble that started deep in his chest and vibrated against her fingers. He began to feather kisses along her jaw, down her throat, all around that spot where he'd bitten her before. When would he do it again? Desire coiled and tightened inside her. "Do it again."

"Sure thing, sugar."

But it was his tongue she felt first, hot and wet. And the bite was sharper this time. So was the pleasure. Her skin felt icy cold and hot at the same time, and desire tightened into an ache. Suddenly, she had to touch him. She ran her hands up his chest. The hair felt soft, the skin smooth. Both sensations provided a delicious contrast to the rock-hard muscles she felt beneath.

"Yes," he murmured as he began to nibble again along the line of her throat. "Touch me."

Encouraged, she ran her palms down his sides and lower over his narrow waist and sharp hip bones, absorbing the hard planes and angles. Each little response he made—a sharp intake of breath when she tried to span his waist, a groan when she moved lower to his thighs—spurred her on. She'd never before received so much enjoyment from merely touching a man. The more she did it, the more she wanted to continue.

To her surprise, her hands seemed to be developing a mind of their own as they moved down and up his thighs, then around to grip his buttocks. And squeeze.

"You're good," he said, gripping her waist and pulling her close so that she felt the hard length of his penis press into her stomach.

This time, her groan mixed with his, and the ache inside of her twisted into a pain. Then he set her back against the tree. "Touch me."

Her hands followed his command and closed around the hard length of him. Once again she marveled at the contrasts—steel hardness covered in velvet. Fascinated, she stroked her hand down, then up. She was about to do it again when he gripped her wrist.

"Am I doing it wrong?" she asked.

For the first time, he wasn't smiling and the look she saw in his eyes wasn't amusement. It was something else, something that shot a little shock wave of heat through her.

"Sugar, you're doing it just right, and if you keep doing it, we won't make it to the hammock."

That would have been perfectly fine with her, but she didn't protest when he drew her hand away and placed it on his waist. "You're really attached to your fantasies, aren't you?"

Now his lips curved just the barest fraction. "You got that right. And I haven't nearly finished collecting data."

She was absolutely sure that her heart skipped a beat as he slowly lowered his mouth again. His lips brushed hers briefly, then retreated until they were barely a breath away. "Let me see. Where was I?"

Before she could think of an answer, he angled his head and pressed his mouth to the base of her throat. Then using both lips and tongue he journeyed lower inch by inch until he reached the valley between her breasts. Then he lingered there as if some flavor had captured him. Tension coiled inside of her again.

His hands lay at the sides of her breasts and his thumbs were still stroking gently, steadily over her nipples. At any moment she expected him to remove one of his thumbs and replace it with his mouth. Just the thought had her nipples growing harder. She was anticipating the way his mouth would feel, but when he finally moved again it was to brush his lips lower. And Lower. Each lick of his tongue, each press of his mouth sent shivers along her nerve endings.

She shuddered and cried out when he pushed his tongue deep into her navel and pinched her nipples at the same instant. She'd never experienced pleasure so sharp or a need so consuming.

"You're so responsive," he murmured as he nipped at her waist. "Better than I ever dreamed."

The words brought their own kind of pleasure. She felt as if she should respond, but her thoughts were focused on what he was doing with his mouth and where he was headed. At least, she thought she knew where he was headed as he released her breasts, lowered to his knees and drew her legs apart. Anticipation streamed through her, and for the second time she was willing to believe that it was half the fun. But she wanted the rest of it, and she wanted it now.

Her voice was a rasp when she said, "I'm ready."

"In a minute. I'm really getting into this data collection."

She wanted to hit him, but she couldn't seem to lift her arms.

And still he took his time, making her wait, making her want, until the tension building inside of her was almost unbearable. She thought she knew what was coming, what it would feel like when his mouth finally reached its destination, but the quick lick of his tongue shot through her like electricity.

She cried out, arching as her arms shot back to grip the bark of the tree.

"I've got you," he murmured as he gripped her thighs to steady her. Then he pulled her closer for a deeper taste, probing first with his tongue and then more deeply with his fingers. The pleasure grew more intense as he penetrated her again and again in a slow, steady motion.

But every time she thought she was close to climaxing, he drew away to trail a line of kisses down her thigh. And then he would start the process all over again.

She wanted to scream but she couldn't find the breath. She wanted him to go on almost as much as she wanted to end the torture he was putting her through.

When he finally stood up and drew her toward the hammock, she would have done anything he wanted. On the way, he grabbed his shorts, removed a condom, and managed to get it on.

"Getting in is always a bit tricky. Turn around."

As soon as she did, he slipped an arm around her waist and positioned her back against his chest. "When I sit, I'm going to pull you into my lap and then we'll tumble in together."

Her legs felt like jelly. If he hadn't had a strong grip on her, Zoë was sure she would have landed fanny first on the ground. As it was, they made it into the hammock without a mishap. He'd been right about the close quarters, she decided. They were lying on their sides, pressed together tight like spoons in a silverware drawer. She should have been uncomfortable, yet she wasn't. He was a solid wall behind her. Their legs were tangled; one of his lay between hers. One of his arms was trapped beneath her, and his free hand was stroking over her hip. She was very aware of his erection pressing hard against her backside, fanning the fire that he'd started inside of her.

"You okay?" he asked.

"No," she said, suddenly annoyed. "I'm not going to

be okay until you're inside of me. No more data collecting." But when she tried to turn, intending to get on top of him, he held her still.

"So help me," she fumed. "You're going to pay for this."

His chuckle rumbled again. "I sure hope so, sugar. But trust me. I've got a plan."

"It better be faster than—" She broke off, distracted when he shifted slightly, lifting the leg that was between hers. "Did I mention that getting in is always a bit tricky?" Then he pushed into her in one long, slow stroke.

"Better?" he murmured against her ear.

She wasn't sure. She wasn't sure she could breathe. He was filling her and the pressure was huge. She drew air in. Maybe. "Yes."

"You don't sound positive. We could try something else."

But when he started to withdraw, she reached behind and clamped a hand on his butt. "No." She didn't think she could stand it if he withdrew. "This is fine."

"*Fine* isn't what I'm after," he murmured. "Let's try this."

He moved his left hand to cover her breast and slid his right one lower until one finger was between her folds and pressing against her clitoris. At the same moment, he withdrew and then pushed in again. The fierce lash of pleasure made her cry out.

"Shh," he murmured, holding her still until she steadied. "Did I hurt you?"

"No," she managed. "Yes. Do it again."

He did, slowly for the first few strokes as if he were waiting for her to get used to him. When her nails dug into his butt again, he steadily increased his rhythm. The pleasure streaming through her grew more intense with every stroke. She knew her climax was close, but he still wasn't moving fast enough, hard enough. She'd never had release build this slowly, this agonizingly. She'd never known a hunger like this. Was this what he'd meant about anticipation?

Desperate, she dug her nails one more time into his butt. "Please. I need—"

He used his mouth on her neck, biting hard on that spot that he'd located before. Then he began to move faster and faster until her orgasm finally erupted in a violent explosion of pleasure.

Even then, he didn't slow the rhythm, and when he cried out with his own release, she climaxed again.

Afterward, he held her close for a long time until the trembling that she couldn't seem to control stopped.

And she let him hold her. There was pleasure, a totally different kind, in lying there in the hammock with his arms holding her tight.

That one small piece of data told her that she was in deep trouble.

5

"WE NEED TO TALK," Jed said.

Ryder turned from the railing of the houseboat where he'd been watching what he could see of Sierra's car disappear up the dirt road in a cloud of dust. The early-morning sky was pale gray with a sliver of silver moon still visible in the sky. "Right now? What time is it?"

"Six o'clock." Jed tried to keep the impatience out of his voice. He'd wanted to talk to Ryder since Zoë had left the afternoon before. Since his friend had been occupied with Sierra, he'd bided his time. But the sense that his time was running out had been growing more urgent since Zoë had left. And he knew from experience to trust his instincts. He handed Ryder one of the mugs of coffee he was holding.

"Thanks. You read my mind." Ryder took a tentative sip, then a long swallow before he narrowed his eyes and studied his friend. "You're up early."

"Didn't sleep much."

Ryder made a grunt that Jed interpreted as sympathy,

then took another long swallow of the coffee. "Give me a minute here. Need the caffeine."

Jed could appreciate that. He was on his second cup. He didn't suppose his old friend had gotten much sleep all weekend. Jed himself hadn't slept much because his thoughts had been filled with Zoë.

It hadn't been merely the lovemaking that had filled his mind whenever he'd closed his eyes and tried to drift off. Although he'd thought about that. A lot. Try as he might, he couldn't shake loose the memory of what she'd tasted like, what she'd felt like—that silky, smooth skin, that slender, athletic body.

Also on his mind had been what had happened afterward when he'd held her…and hadn't wanted to let her go. Even now his body was recalling the pleasure he'd felt simply lying there holding her close. He'd drifted off then, and he wasn't sure how long he'd slept. But when Zoë had awakened him, she'd been all business, all tightly wound nerves.

He hadn't been able to resist the urge to loosen her up again. He'd wanted to experience once more what it felt like to make her come. Unfortunately, his attempt had tumbled them both out of the hammock.

She'd laughed. They both had, like idiots. And strangely enough it had been the image of Zoë McNamara, sitting next to him on the ground and laughing that had most persistently haunted his thoughts during the night.

He'd never heard her laugh before and he wanted to

hear that rich, delightful sound again almost as much as he wanted to make love to her again.

But he couldn't follow up on either desire. Jed took a long swallow of coffee, and this time he tasted the bitterness. It suited his current mood. Pursuing any kind of further relationship with Zoë McNamara was impossible as long as he was a "dead" man.

If the gut feeling he'd been experiencing that Bailey Montgomery had spotted him at that big D.C. party hadn't been enough to spur him to action, the time he'd spent with Zoë certainly had.

"Shit," Ryder said. "This coffee sucks. It's been—what?—ten years since we shared an apartment in college, and your coffee hasn't improved?"

Turning, Jed raised an eyebrow as he studied his friend. "Well, your taste buds are functioning. Are the brain cells up and running yet?"

Ryder ran the fingers of one hand through his hair, glaring down at the mug in his hand. "Making a decent cup of coffee isn't rocket science. I don't know anyone who's a better shot with a rifle than you are." He waved his free hand. "Except for me, there's no one who can match you at finessing the information highway to find out anything you want to know, whether it's classified or not. You know Shakespeare's plays like the back of your hand. My God, you're even a brilliant tactical fisherman. If you ever want to give up government work, you can probably get your own show on the fishing channel. I can't see how you can screw up fixing a simple cup of coffee day after day."

"Consistency is one of my finer qualities," Jed said with a grin. "And if you're through with your rant, I'd like to get down to business. I've been imposing on your hospitality for two weeks now, and I know that you've put in a good many hours but so far we haven't even gotten the scent of who framed me for Frank Medici's murder."

"Not true," Ryder said. "We know that Agent Bailey Montgomery executed the hit. She may be in on the frame."

"Hell, I told you that much. But she didn't execute the hit alone. It was a sharpshooter who got me in the shoulder. Her bullet was the second one." Jed reminded him. "In any case, she's the one person who might know something that would help me."

Ryder turned and studied him again. His eyes and the set of his face told Jed that either the words or the coffee had done the trick.

"I'm thinking that it's time I took a more proactive role in this," Jed said.

"You've decided to rise from the dead?" Ryder asked.

Jed rubbed the back of his neck. "I've got this feeling that I may have already risen. I haven't told you because you've been busy with Sierra. And I've been trying to come up with a strategy."

Ryder's eyes narrowed. "Haven't told me what?"

"Bailey Montgomery may have spotted me at that D.C. party when I was supposed to be helping you guard Sierra." He'd been stationed on the patio at the back of the Langford house right outside the room where Sierra was supposed to be meeting with the vice president. Someone had knocked him out. He hadn't been out for more than a few minutes but it had been enough time for a killer to kidnap Sierra. It had certainly been enough time for someone passing by to get a good look at him.

"I should have insisted that you wear one of your disguises."

Jed's brows shot up. "And how would we have explained that to Sierra and her sisters and their significant others and Zoë? Besides, we didn't plan on my being knocked out."

"Right." Ryder sighed. "Why didn't you mention the possibility that you'd been spotted before?"

"Because I don't have anything to go on besides a gut feeling. I got it again when we left your little engagement shindig the other night at the Blue Pepper. I think I spotted a car following us—a dark-colored SUV or a van. I lost it easily enough, so I can't be sure, but I haven't been able to get rid of the feeling that my time is running out."

"Great," Ryder said. "I know you well enough— what your gut instinct is telling you is probably right. That means we have to make some kind of a move." He took another swallow of his coffee. "That SUV—that's why you did all that fancy driving on the way back here that night, isn't it?"

Jed grinned at him. "I thought you were too distracted with Sierra in the backseat to notice."

Ryder ran a hand through his hair again. "Yeah, I was, or I would have figured it out sooner. But if you're right and someone saw you with Sierra and me, they're going to pursue that connection. Good thing no one can trace me to this place. Even if they could, it's next to impossible to find without specific directions."

Ryder took another swallow of coffee. "If you think Bailey Montgomery is your best source of information, please don't tell me that you're just going to walk into her office and ask her."

Jed smiled slowly. "It's a tempting thought. But I was thinking of a more conservative move—to start off with at least. I'm thinking we might break into her office and search it—her desk, her hard drive."

Ryder's eyes narrowed thoughtfully. "You're talking about breaking into the CIA headquarters in Langley? It'd be a challenge."

Just the kind of challenge that Ryder would enjoy. Jed was banking on that. Still deep in thought, Ryder took a long sip of his coffee, grimaced and then spat it out over the railing. "Shit. I can't drink this. We're going to finish this conversation in the galley."

Jed followed him down the short flight of stairs. The kitchen was small and well equipped with shiny pots and pans hanging off hooks. Ryder filled the teakettle, rinsed out the French-press pot and measured coffee into it.

"Gage Sinclair might be willing to help us," Jed said.

Ryder frowned in concentration. "Gage Sinclair. If

it's the same man I'm thinking of, he doesn't work at the CIA anymore."

Jed shook his head. "No. But we worked together on a couple of assignments, and I got him out of a messy situation about seven years ago on a job we did together in Jordan. He got shot up pretty bad and lost a leg but it could have been a lot worse. Since then, he's gotten out of fieldwork."

"He's doing private consulting and security work here in D.C.," Ryder said. "I've run into him a few times. He even invited me to work on a case with him a year ago. I liked him, and he's good at what he does. We'd be rivals if he weren't primarily doing contract work for the CIA."

"If anyone would know the ins and outs of CIA head-quarters, he would," Jed said.

"Can you trust him?"

"Yeah. He's a good man. Even if he believes I killed Frank, he'll figure he owes me at least one favor. Plus, I know him well enough to suspect there's a reason why he left the CIA. It wasn't just because of his injuries. He wasn't entirely happy with the CIA. But he still consults for them, so he'll have a pass. He probably knows the building like the back of his hand. I'll set up a meet as soon as possible."

"Set it up at the Blue Pepper."

Jed thought for a minute. The Blue Pepper was a very popular Georgetown watering hole that drew not only on the academics from the university but also on staffers from the hill. "Why there?"

Ryder glanced at him. "It's public, you've been there before, and I'm familiar with all the entrances and exits. I'll put two men on you as soon as you set up the meet. If you're right and someone, perhaps Agent Montgomery, suspects you've risen from the dead, she may also suspect that you'll contact me or Gage. We'd be in your file. So Gage may be followed. If he is, I'll know it."

"Okay."

Ryder thought some more. "You'll wear a disguise."

Jed grinned at him. "Of course."

Ryder smiled. "Which persona are you going to assume this time?"

"I'm thinking of turning myself into Ethan Blair, British diplomat, until this is over. He has a slight accent and very expensive taste in food, wine and clothes. He's one of my favorites."

Ryder shook his head. "How many different men have you turned yourself into over the years?"

"A baker's dozen, give or take a couple." Then Jed's smile faded. "I'll register under Ethan's name at the Woodbridge Hotel, and you won't have to worry about anyone following me back here. You and Sierra will be safer if I'm not around."

Ryder nodded. "I'll keep two men on you. But even using a disguise, the meeting with Gage is risky."

"He's my best bet to get us into that office. Bailey Montgomery is a good operative. And she's meticulous. I'm betting that she's kept some kind of file. I wouldn't be surprised if she has a file on Frank Medici, too. I want to know who killed him and why. I was just starting to check into that when I agreed to meet Bailey down in Colombia. All I need is a thread. Then I can start pulling it to figure out exactly what is going on."

Ryder gave him a brief nod. "Looks like we've got a plan."

Jed smiled. "Yeah. I'll get in touch with Gage today."

"Say as little as possible over the phone."

"Right. I'll fax him the details."

As the teakettle began to shriek, Ryder turned back to the stove and busied himself making coffee.

Jed knew from experience that his friend was in mulling-it-over mode. Right now he was covering all the angles that Jed had outlined in his own mind in the wee hours of the morning. So he was surprised when Ryder turned back, coffee mug in hand, cleared his throat, and said, "About Zoë McNamara."

After a moment, Jed said, "What about her?"

"What I want to know is…" Ryder let the partial sentence hang as he shifted his gaze away. He took a sip of his coffee and then a bigger swallow. "I couldn't help but noticing…she was here yesterday for a couple of hours." Finally, he met Jed's eyes directly. "Hell, I'm no good at this."

To Jed's astonishment, Ryder's face had turned red. Ryder Kane was the most unflappable man he'd ever known. He'd personally seen his friend face a bullet without so much as blinking, let alone allowing his blood pressure to fluctuate.

Ryder cleared his throat. "Zoë is a good friend of Sierra's. And Sierra feels very protective toward her. And she's…" As his sentence trailed off, Ryder raised a hand. "I know it's none of my business, but Sierra would be very unhappy if Zoë got hurt."

"Zoë's a big girl."

"Exactly. That's what I told Sierra, but she made me promise to… Shit. I told her it was none of our business if the two of you—do whatever the two of you want to do. But she wanted me to say something." He picked up the mug and drained it. "Hell, I'm still trying to get used to all the stuff that goes along with being involved with one person. You don't just have a relationship with a woman. You get the whole package—friends, work associates, relatives. And the relatives' friends and significant others. Forget I brought it up."

"Done," Jed said. "But if it will make Sierra feel any better, you can tell her that as far as Zoë's concerned, our relationship is over."

"Over?"

Jed nodded. "She as much as told me so herself. When she left yesterday, she told me she really appreciated my letting her sort of burn away all that sexual frustration she'd been feeling."

Ryder's brows shot up. "She actually said that?"

"Yeah." Jed smiled slowly. "And then she shook my hand just as if we'd concluded a little business meeting. Can you picture it? She is so damn cute."

"NIGHT AFTER TOMORROW at the Blue Pepper," Gage said, making a note on his calendar. "I'll wait for the fax."

Replacing the phone, Gage Sinclair leaned back in his chair and stretched out his good leg. The little hum of excitement that had begun zinging through his blood the moment he'd heard Jed Calhoun's voice was something that he'd missed.

Gage had cut the conversation very short. No details, he'd warned. And no name. Jed was sending the info in a fax.

Gage Sinclair didn't trust phones—neither the cellular nor land varieties. He didn't much like e-mail, either. He was more aware than most of how difficult it was to eliminate all traces of those little missives once they were sent. In the kind of work he did, he knew full well how vulnerable every form of communication was to eavesdropping. George Orwell had gotten it right in *1984.* Big Brother *was* watching. And listening.

His lips curved in a smile. Hell, he made a living watching and listening. And he'd still be doing it for the CIA if he hadn't lost his leg.

No, that wasn't quite right. Part of his reason for resigning from the CIA was that if he'd stayed, he'd have eventually had to work under Hadley Richards. And he just didn't like the man.

He'd spent too many years in the field, he supposed. In that kind of work, you learned to size up anyone you worked with quickly and you either trusted them or you didn't. He'd worked with some of the best agents around—Jed Calhoun, Frank Medici. They were men he'd trusted with his life.

Hadley Richards was a paper-pushing politician who, because he played all the right games and had influential connections, would be the next director of the CIA. Politicians were necessary, Gage supposed. But they were hard to trust. He'd seen the writing on the wall concerning Richards and he'd gotten out early. He was too independent to work for someone he couldn't respect.

Shifting his gaze to his right, he glanced out at a world-class view. All in all, it had been a good move for him. From his fifth-floor office, he could see the Washington Mall, and in the distance, the Washington Monument. Private consulting work paid very well. He was his own boss, the view was better than the one he'd had in his office at CIA headquarters, and best of all, he got to pick and choose his cases. If he had any regrets it was that he was still alone. Not that a single man "batching" it in D.C. had to be lonely. But he'd always thought that once he retired from the field, he'd find the perfect woman and settle down.

Maybe the perfect woman didn't exist. He'd thought he'd found one once, but it had been the wrong time and the wrong place.

He turned back to his desk. A man shouldn't complain when he was lucky enough to enjoy his work and be good at it. And now he had a challenging case.

He hadn't had to think twice about taking Jed Calhoun's. Nor had he needed any of the information Jed was currently faxing him to make his decision. Jed Calhoun was a trusted friend as well as the man who'd saved his life. He'd never believed that Jed had killed Frank Medici. And Jed hadn't been taken out, as had been the word. That was the good news.

The bad news—and Gage had discovered there was always a downside to every piece of news he received— was that Jed had been framed for the murder of Frank Medici. And by appearing again in D.C., he ran the risk of being taken out for real this time.

Another reason he'd taken the case was that he would have a chance, working with Jed, to find out what had really happened to Frank Medici. He'd admired Frank nearly as much as he admired Jed. When he'd thought that they were both dead, he'd not only been saddened, but he'd thought it was a sad day for the CIA.

There was nothing that fascinated Gage more than a good mystery. And from the moment he'd heard about Frank Medici's death, he'd suspected that it was just that—a classic whodunit waiting to be solved. What had happened to Jed Calhoun had stunk to high heaven of a frame.

Oh, Jed might have been assigned to take Frank out if that had been deemed necessary by the higher-ups and he might have even carried out the hit. But not for money and certainly not for some drug cartel.

Jed Calhoun was a straight arrow, a Boy Scout almost.

The story had just never fit, which had led Gage to wonder who was behind Frank Medici's death and why.

The war on drugs was a dirty business. It was being waged in many cases by people who didn't really want to win because the profits in the illegal trade of drugs were huge—to everyone involved.

Rising, Gage went to his window. Some of those involved in reaping the profits held high government positions, and they would do a lot to keep their involvement a secret.

The other thing that intrigued him was that finding out the true story behind Frank Medici's death and keeping Jed Calhoun alive were going to present almost impossible challenges.

As his fax machine began to whir, Gage smiled again. It had been a long time since he'd come up against an impossible challenge, and the last time it had cost him a leg. But, one leg and all his brains were intact, he thought, as he lifted a sheet out of his fax machine and began to read.

"I'VE HEARD a disturbing rumor."

Bailey Montgomery closed the file on her desk and glanced up to meet the gaze of her most immediate superior at the CIA, Hadley Richards. "Had" to his friends and a favored few of his subordinates.

He closed the door behind him with a little snap.

Bailey wasn't one of the favored few. She'd worked under "Had" for nearly a year, and he was still Mr. Richards to her. Go figure. Bailey watched him stroll to her desk and make a ritual out of sitting down, pressing the crease in his slacks and lifting them slightly to cut down on wrinkles. Once he was seated, he proceeded to adjust his cuffs.

Hadley Richards was a tall, handsome man in his early fifties who was always meticulously dressed and normally had charm oozing out of his pores. Not that he'd ever wasted any of it on her. In fact, he seemed to check it at the door whenever he entered her office. He was also a man she neither underestimated nor completely trusted.

Since she'd known him, he'd been playing the old-boy network very skillfully to ensure he was on the fast track to becoming the next director. He would probably achieve his goal since he had the right political connections. His father-in-law was the President's National Security Advisor. And it didn't hurt that his wife was richer than a goddess and the current CEO at McManus Pharmaceuticals.

"Well, aren't you going to ask me about the rumor?" Had asked.

Arching one brow, she set down her gold pen and smiled at him. "I'm confident that you're going to enlighten me any second now."

He returned her smile—a slight curve of lips that wasn't echoed in his eyes.

Hadley Richards didn't like her. She wasn't sure if his dislike sprang out of the fact that he didn't believe women belonged in the CIA or whether he feared that she was competing with him. Or perhaps the formal way he treated her was due to the fact that she'd made it clear early in their relationship that she wasn't going to take a tumble with him between the sheets. Had's reputation as a womanizer was firmly established. He was usually discreet. Sometimes, there was gossip, as there had been six months ago when the rumors had circulated that he'd been "seeing" one of the new data analysts, a young woman named Zoë McNamara. But when she'd quickly resigned, the talk had stopped.

"It's about that assignment I asked you to handle in Bogotá six months ago," he said. "Someone has spotted your quarry back here in D.C."

Bailey's stomach clenched, but her gaze remained steady. "That's impossible." Ever since she'd spotted Jed Calhoun at that trendy party at Millie Langford's house two weeks ago, she'd been waiting for this. But Had must have received his news secondhand, so he couldn't be certain. If *he'd* spotted Jed at that party, as she had, he would have been in her office the next day. "The man you sent me to Bogotá to kill is dead."

"You know that party that Millie Langford threw two weeks ago to honor my wife for receiving the President's Humanitarian Award?"

"Yes."

"Well, my source thinks our so-called dead man was there."

Bailey kept her gaze and her voice steady. "Your source is mistaken."

"I've been checking. There's no official record of the man's death."

She shrugged and sent him another smile. "We're talking about Colombia. Records get lost, or more likely, they never get filed. I was there in the alley. I arranged the hit. You'll have to take my word for it. Or the shooter's. His report is in the file. He's the marksman you insisted I take with me."

"I spoke with him. He says that you insisted on a shot to the shoulder."

Bailey's stomach knotted even tighter. "Because I wanted to finish the job myself and make sure there was no mistake. I shot him and let me assure you that he's dead."

For a moment Hadley Richards merely studied her with a slight frown on his face. She knew exactly what he saw. She'd worked very hard to cultivate a specific image on the job. She saw a hairstylist once a month to keep her straight blond hair at a perfect length, one that she could tie at the nape of her neck when she worked out or let fall straight to a spot just below her chin when she was in the office. Her manicurist kept her nails short and covered with a clear polish. And she was wearing her typical uniform, a conservative suit—today's had a pinstripe running through it. The only personal indulgences on the job were the gold hoops she wore in her ears and the red silk blouse.

Finally, Had nodded curtly and rose from his chair. "If anything changes, if you hear anything, notify me immediately."

"Yes, Mr. Richards," she said as he moved out of her office. Then she wadded up the piece of paper she'd been meticulously taking notes on and hurled it at the door. The act was childish she knew. But the man was beginning to really annoy her.

Worse, he was beginning to worry her. Not that he hadn't before. He'd been worrying her for six months, ever since he'd walked into her office and handed her the reports that "proved" Jed Calhoun had murdered Frank Medici for the Vidal drug cartel. They sure as hell had made Jed Calhoun look guilty.

But her gut instinct had told her that Jed Calhoun hadn't killed Frank.

Bailey had known Frank Medici personally. They'd even dated for a while when he was in between assignments. She had a hunch that was why Hadley had assigned her to handle the Jed Calhoun matter. Hadley Richards knew people and he knew how to play them. She was pretty sure he'd tried to play her.

He'd given her the assignment of contacting Jed to meet with Frank and deliver an urgent message that someone in the Vidal cartel might be on to him. So she'd been the one to send Jed Calhoun into that bar. When Hadley had presented her with the evidence of Jed's guilt, he'd told her he'd recommended her for the job of taking Jed out. And Jed hadn't suspected a thing. It was a very neat plan. Send one of Frank Medici's old lovers to take out his killer, someone who'd sent that killer to the meeting that had cost Frank his life, and you could really up your chances of getting the job done.

What Hadley couldn't have known was that Jed Calhoun had been one of the agents that Frank had most admired. He'd talked about Jed all the time, about what a straight arrow he was.

After pushing away from her desk, Bailey walked to the wad of paper, picked it up and dropped it neatly in the wastebasket as she moved toward the window. The late-afternoon sun sent long shadows sprawling across the parking lot below her. Her gaze moved quickly to the trees beyond. There was a small area with picnic tables for office workers who wanted to take their lunch breaks outside in good weather. Her office didn't have one of the best views, nor did it have a corner window, but she liked it.

For some reason, looking out on the small picnic area helped her to center herself and think. Evidently, Hadley Richards had been wrong about her. She hadn't gotten the job done, and now she could only hope to hell that she hadn't been wrong about Jed Calhoun.

But the past couldn't be changed. She had to stick to the present. Hadley Richards only suspected that Jed Calhoun was alive and back in D.C. So she still had the advantage. She *knew* that Jed would be meeting Gage Sinclair at the Blue Pepper tonight.

Once she'd spotted him at that party, she'd taken some precautions. There were two men Jed Calhoun was likely to contact: Ryder Kane or Gage Sinclair. She hadn't been able to tap Ryder's phone. The man's security setup was impregnable. But she had managed to get a tap on Gage's phone. Yesterday it had paid off. They'd been careful in the conversation. But then, Gage Sinclair had always been a very careful man.

She wondered if he remembered her at all. The first time she'd met him face-to-face was eight years ago. She'd been twenty, going into her senior year of college and he'd come to her school on a recruiting visit. She'd been so impressed that she'd done what she could to find out more about him. Gage Sinclair had had a very distinguished career with the CIA. He was not only a brilliant analyst, but he was also one of their best field agents. She supposed, looking back, that she'd developed a sort of crush on him, and the fact that he was a handsome, older man probably only facilitated her feelings. Bailey nearly smiled at the memory. Gage Sinclair was the reason she'd joined the CIA, and during her training, he'd been her mentor. He was the man who'd told her always to rely on her instincts.

She hoped to God they hadn't failed her where Jed Calhoun was concerned.

Tonight she'd have her chance to get to Jed Calhoun before Hadley did. She had to talk to him. Her job and his life, and perhaps her own, depended on that.

6

THE SUN ON THE BACK of her neck was warm and soothing. Zoë sighed contentedly. The hammock wasn't moving and she concluded vaguely that the breeze must have let up. She was alone. But Jed was near. She could feel his fingers, featherlight, moving from the base of her neck, down her back. The slow stroking of his hand, languidly seducing, lazily arousing, brought sleepy, exquisite pleasure. With a little moan, she arched her shoulders into the gentle caress of that magical touch. She was floating, suspended.

A faint sound—a ringing—pulled at her, but she fought it. She wanted the sensations she was experiencing to continue. Endlessly. She had no cares, no worries, no—

The ring was sharper this time, and it had Zoë's head snapping up. Her hand connected with something, and she heard a flutter of…something. She blinked, but her mind was so fuzzy, so disoriented, that she wasn't sure where she was.

Another ring.

Zoë looked around and tried to focus. She wasn't in

the hammock. Disappointment rolled through her. Reality crashed back in. She was in her office. And she'd just sent a pile of note cards slithering helter-skelter across the floor. Damn. An hour's work was destroyed in one fell swoop. She dropped her head into her hands.

It was all Jed Calhoun's fault.

When the phone rang yet another time, she picked it up. "Zoë McNamara here."

There was no response on the other end. Whoever had called had been transferred to voice mail. Had it been Jed? She pressed the caller ID button, saw Sierra's name and made an effort to swallow her disappointment.

Jed hadn't called her. Not the night they'd made love, not yesterday and not today. It was ridiculous for her to feel so bummed about that. They'd had an agreement.

She had to put aside the fact that the one-time-only event had been a bad idea. Making love with him in that hammock had only increased her appetite for him.

It hadn't worked the way she'd planned. Not at all. When it came to men, nothing ever did.

Dropping her hands to the desk, she fisted them and shoved down on the bubble of panic that was expanding in her stomach. Opening the top drawer of her desk, she took out her Jed Calhoun notebook and flipped it open to a fresh page. Her experience analyzing research had taught her to face the truth head-on.

Number one: She wanted to make love to Jed Calhoun again. No use lying about that. Her dreams, along with her waking thoughts, were filled with him even more than they'd been before.

Number two: Arranging another "event" with Jed probably wouldn't solve her problem. It might even make it worse. What if her appetite for him increased again? There were cases in the narrative data she'd collected where instant and high-potency chemistry between two people never burned out. It lasted for years and years. She'd recently interviewed a couple in their sixties who'd sworn that what was between them was "hotter than ever."

Number three: She needed another solution. Her theory that making love with him one time would solve her problem had been wrong. It was time to try something else. That's what researchers and analysts did. She glanced at the cards strewn across the floor and at the blank sheet of paper on her desk. *Work.* It had always been her salvation before. She'd just throw herself back into it and eventually, the memory of Jed Calhoun would fade.

It had to.

She was about to rise to gather up the note cards when a sharp knock sounded on her door.

"Zoë, are you in there?"

Before Zoë could reply, the door opened and Sierra strode in. "Are you all right? I've tried twice to get you on the phone. I—" Sierra's voice broke off as she gazed at the floor. "Are you all right?"

"I'm fine," Zoë said.

Sierra glanced around the room. "I don't think so.

You're not answering your phone, and I've never seen your office like this."

"I have a lot on my mind."

Sierra sat down in the chair facing Zoë's and said, "This is about Jed Calhoun, isn't it?"

Zoë folded her hands on the desk and concentrated hard. Lying wasn't one of her strengths. "That's over. Jed and I just decided to act on our mutual attraction for one another. Both of us have other priorities right now and the chemistry between us was getting in our way. Now it's finished."

Sierra's eyes narrowed.

The lie hadn't worked. Zoë could sense it, but she managed to hold Sierra's gaze and she didn't blush.

"If you don't want to talk about it, that's fine. But I don't know what I would have done if I hadn't had my sisters to talk to when I first met Ryder. Did you know that I kissed him in the bar of the Blue Pepper before I ever knew his name? I just kissed him—a perfect stranger."

Zoë bit on her bottom lip, glanced at her phone and then finally said, "It's been two days and he hasn't called."

Sierra frowned. "Jed's life is complicated right now. He moved out of Ryder's houseboat yesterday. And Ryder can't or won't tell me where he's gone."

Zoë's heart sank. "I really didn't expect him to call."

"But you're having second thoughts about that. I can tell, and it's my fault. I encouraged you to go after him."

Zoë met Sierra's eyes. "This is not your fault. It was

my decision, and I don't regret it." Even as she said the words, Zoë realized they were true. How could she ever regret the time she'd spent with Jed?

"Well, I'm going to see if I can get some more information out of Ryder. In the meantime—" Sierra paused to glance around the office "—I think you need a girls' night out."

"I don't know, I—"

"My sisters and I and two of Natalie's friends are gathering at Rory's place first. Rory's fiancé, Hunter, owns this exclusive lingerie shop and Rory is bringing samples from the new line to show us. Jed Calhoun isn't the only man out there."

Zoë opened her mouth, but Sierra hurried on. "C'mon. What have you got to lose? There's nothing like some really sexy underwear to build up your confidence."

"Sexy underwear?"

"Really sexy."

Zoë thought about how new underwear had been one of the things she'd intended to purchase before she'd even approached Jed in the first place.

Sierra rose and moved toward the door. "Rory will explain everything. She swears that the main reason she captured Hunter's heart was a red thong." Sierra opened the door. "C'mon. It'll be fun."

Zoë glanced down. "I'm not really dressed to go out."

"Rory will lend you something, and afterward, we're having dinner at the Blue Pepper." She grinned at Zoë. "Who knows? The love of your life could be waiting for you there right now! That's where I first met Ryder."

What *did* she have to lose? Zoë thought as she rose and followed Sierra out the door.

THE FACT THAT the Blue Pepper was one of Georgetown's most popular bistros was confirmed for Jed as he entered the restaurant. His gaze followed a waiter with a loaded tray climbing the short flight of stairs that led from the crowded bar to the main dining area. The tables were nearly all taken. A glance to his right told him that the tables on the patio were filled, too. Above the noise of the conversations buzzing around him, he could hear that the band was playing jazz.

George, a gentle giant of a man and one of the owners, was swamped with customers at the bar, and his partner, Rad, a small man with flamboyant taste in clothes and hairstyles, was greeting guests at the reservation desk. The two men were partners in life as well as business, and they seemed to make a perfect team. The waiting area was so crowded with customers that Jed had to elbow his way through them.

He'd been here once before with Ryder and Sierra and her sisters, and he'd gone along with Ryder's suggestion that he meet Gage here because he was familiar with the place and he could depend on it being crowded. There was a slim chance that someone might be watching Gage, and it was always easier to disappear into a crowd.

When he finally reached the reservation desk, Rad was sweet-talking an impatient-looking customer. Tonight, Rad was a picture in black and white—white hair, black silk shirt and slacks set off with a black-and-white striped tie. The man had a sharp eye for both people and fashion, and a knack for remembering faces. This would be the first test of his disguise, and it would be a tough one.

"…very busy tonight," Rad was saying. "But I think I can fit you in on the patio in about forty-five minutes if you'd like to wait in the bar."

"Okay. But don't forget I'm there," said the impatient man.

"Never," Rad promised with a reassuring smile and then scribbled something in the reservation book.

Jed waited for Rad to glance up at him. In the kind of work he'd done for the government, he'd had quite a bit of experience with donning disguises. He wondered what Rad would think of Ethan Blair.

Rad glanced up at him. "Yes?"

"Ethan Blair. I have a reservation for two at eight o'clock. I requested a table near the railing on the upper level."

Something flashed into Rad's eyes, and Jed saw with relief that it was interest and not recognition. Rad had an eye for fashion, and his gaze swept over Jed as he grabbed two menus. Jed knew exactly what the man was seeing—the silk shirt and tie, the Italian-designed suit. He'd temporarily dyed his hair black and had it trimmed at the men's salon at the Woodbridge Hotel where he'd also gotten a manicure. He'd purchased the gold pinkie ring he wore in the hotel's gift shop. The Woodbridge, the hotel where he'd elected to stay for the next few days, was located close to Georgetown and boasted several exits. He'd picked up the glasses—which Jed felt added the perfect touch to the disguise—at one of those chains that guarantees one-hour service.

Rad's eyes returned to his face, and Jed knew that he was noting the single diamond he wore in his right ear. Often it was the little things that meant the most in a disguise. With his knack for sizing up people, Rad would never associate an earring or a pinkie ring with Jed Calhoun.

Rad beamed a smile at him. "You're a Brit, right?"

Jed nodded. "The accent gave me away?"

"The clothes, too," Rad said as he began leading the way to the table. "American men have never developed the knack for dressing well. I love the tie, by the way. Mind telling me where you got it?"

"Harrods," Jed said.

"Figured as much," Rad said. "I'm very fond of ties. I suppose the shopping over there is better, too."

"Much," Jed agreed amiably as they reached the table.

Rad nodded knowingly. "Now if you'll just describe your friend to me?"

"He'll ask for me by name," Jed said.

As Rad hurried away, Jed picked up one of the menus, but even as he did, he had the peculiar sensation that someone was watching him. As his muscles began to tense, he willed them to relax.

There was no one who could have followed him. After Ryder had dropped him off at Union Station, he'd taken a series of taxis before he'd arrived at the Wood-bridge, and he'd made the same maneuvers coming to the Blue Pepper. It had to be Gage. Evidently, his old friend was already here.

Setting down the menu, he slowly scanned the crowd in the restaurant. Gage was a tall man with a rangy build, dark hair and intelligent eyes. He had a knack for being able to fade into a crowd, but if you met him in a dark alley, he was someone you wouldn't want to mess with.

It had been three years since he'd last seen his old friend, but none of the men he saw in the waiting area earned a second glance. Casually, he shifted his gaze to the bar and instantly, his eyes collided with Zoë McNamara's.

For a moment, he froze as questions and emotions tangled inside of him. What was she doing here? Had she recognized him? Even more disturbing to him were the feelings that seeing her had immediately sparked.

Desire was paramount. Making love to her hadn't done a thing to dampen what he felt for her. In fact, it had turned what might have been simple attraction into a craving. In the two days that they had been apart, he'd decided something. He was going to have Zoë again, but not until he'd cleared his name. In the meantime, he wasn't going to go anywhere near her because, if he did, he would put her in grave danger.

He also felt a hint of surprise. There was something different about her. She was wearing her hair down, and it fell in a shining sweep to her shoulders. The clothes were different, too. She was wearing a lace-edged top that looked more like lingerie than something a woman would wear out to a bar. Was she meeting a man?

Jealousy twisted in his gut like a claw. A quick look assured him that she was completely surrounded by women. He recognized Sierra first, then her sisters, and two other women he'd met at Ryder's engagement party a week ago. Only then did the twisting in his gut ease.

How long had he been staring at her? He knew it had likely only been for a moment. But she was looking at him as if he were something smeared on a slide. Did she recognize him?

No. The disguise was good. Rad hadn't penetrated it close-up, so surely she couldn't have from a distance.

Slowly, Jed shifted his gaze back to the reservation desk. Gage stood at one side talking to Rad. *Keep your mind on business,* Jed reminded himself. If everything went as planned, Gage would join him at the table, hand over an envelope with the floor plan of Bailey Montgomery's office building, and any other information Ryder might need. Then they would have a friendly drink together and each go their separate ways.

But Gage didn't come toward the table. Instead, he made his way into the crowded bar. Jed's hand fisted in his lap. Something was definitely wrong.

7

"Zoë?"

With a little start, Zoë blinked and shifted her gaze to Sierra who sat on the bar stool next to hers. "What?"

Sierra leaned close and pitched her voice to be heard over the din of conversation bombarding them from all sides. "George asked if you want more wine."

It was only then that Zoë noticed that the bartender was holding a bottle over her nearly empty glass.

"I know you have a preference for crisp white wines, and this one is a very good vintage," George said.

"No, thanks." Zoë tried to gather her thoughts.

"You all right?" Sierra asked when George moved away. "You were a thousand miles away."

"I'm fine," Zoë said. But she hadn't been a thousand miles away. She'd just been totally focused on a man who sat at a table in the main dining room only a few yards away.

She wasn't sure how long she'd been staring at him before Sierra had pulled her attention back. She'd noticed him earlier when he'd been talking to Rad, the

Blue Pepper's other owner, at the reservation desk, and she'd felt a strange sort of recognition—as if she'd met him before. Her first thought was that he'd been one of the many single men she'd interviewed when she'd been collecting data for Sierra's study.

But she would have remembered him. Just looking at him had a lick of lust moving through her. Sexy and elegant were the words that had come to mind as she'd watched the stranger follow Rad to the table. The purposeful way he moved in the impeccably tailored suit reminded her a little of the image she'd created in her mind of Lucifer—all that easy sophistication on the outside that didn't quite mask the aura of danger beneath.

She'd sensed a similar contrast in Jed. Although he could in no way be described as elegant on the outside. No. Jed had rough edges, and this man epitomized the word *smooth.* But Jed Calhoun definitely had that same hint of danger hiding beneath the beach boy façade.

In a sense, the two men were very like Lucifer in that respect. Lucifer. How interesting, she thought suddenly. After spending six months filling her notebooks with fantasies about the superspy, she hadn't spared him more than a passing thought since she'd met Jed Calhoun.

Then she noticed another similarity between Jed and the stranger. Glasses aside, in profile, they both had the same strong chin, straight nose and the kind of cheekbones that one saw on a warrior's face.

She lifted her wineglass and finished the last swallow. Zoë was dimly aware of the separate conversations going on behind her. When they'd arrived at the Blue Pepper, they'd been joined by two of the Gibbs sisters' friends, Sophie McBride and Mac Wainwright.

Sierra and Mac, who both taught at Georgetown, were talking about faculty politics while Sophie Wainwright was telling Natalie and Rory Gibbs all about the latest art pieces that had arrived in her antique shop. Zoë knew she should turn and join in one of the conversations, but for some reason, she couldn't seem to pull either her mind or her gaze away from the stranger at the table.

When he turned slowly just then and met her gaze, Zoë felt that same little shock of recognition she'd felt when she'd first seen him. This time it was so intense that her mind drained of all thought. At the same time, she could feel her whole body become aware of him. It was almost as if he'd touched her and sparked a little flame deep inside of her. For an instant, everything around her—the conversations, the music from the patio, even the people lined up three deep around the bar—faded. She could have sworn that she and the stranger were totally alone in the restaurant.

"Zoë?"

From very far away, Zoë could hear someone calling her name.

"Zoë, are you sure you're all right?"

Zoë tried to focus, but it wasn't until the man glanced away that she could turn to face Sierra again.

"I'm fine," she managed. But she wasn't fine. Her

skin felt icy and hot at the same time. She leaned closer to Sierra. "Look at that man over there at the table near the railing."

Sierra shifted her gaze. "Handsome." Then she grinned and nudged her elbow into Zoë's arm. "Zoë McNamara, you're actually ogling a man!"

"Of course, she is," Rory said, moving closer. "Wearing the right kind of lingerie can change your whole attitude toward men."

"I'm not ogling," Zoë protested. "Exactly." But wasn't that exactly what she was doing? And she didn't think that it had anything to do with the sexy red lace panties that Rory had insisted she wear under the borrowed jeans and the lacy camisole top. She was afraid the ogling had everything to do with the man.

"Where is he?" Rory asked.

"Over there at the table near the railing." Zoë moved her head in the stranger's direction. She didn't want to point. "Doesn't he remind you of someone?"

Sierra studied him for a moment. "James Bond—the one played by Pierce Brosnan."

"I don't mean a movie star. I'm thinking of a real person," Zoë said.

"Haven't a clue." Sierra shifted her gaze to her sisters and their friends. "Look at the man sitting at the table near the railing. Zoë wants to know who he reminds you of."

All of the women studied him for a moment.

"I don't know," Natalie said. "But those glasses look sexy on him."

"Definitely," Sierra said.

Zoë never quite got used to how pretty Sierra's sisters were and how different. Natalie, the oldest, was a redhead and a D.C. cop.

"I vote for the guy who plays the father on *The OC*." Rory, the middle sister, was short, dark-haired, and a freelance writer.

"Peter Gallagher," Sierra said. "Yes, I can see the resemblance in the cheekbones, but the man we're ogling has a firmer jawline. I still vote for James Bond."

"I say Mark Wahlberg," Sophie said. "He's hot."

"Mark or this guy?" Natalie asked.

"Both," Rory and Sophie answered in unison.

"I'm thinking of someone who's not a movie star," Zoë said.

"Okay." Mac studied him for a minute. "In profile, especially in the nose and the jawline, I think he looks a bit like Ryder's friend, Jed Calhoun."

"No," Sierra said. "He's too…stiff. Look at that posture."

"You're right about the posture, but I think he looks a little like Jed, too," Zoë said. And she was hoping that the resemblance was what had triggered her intense reaction to the man. "Every one of us is supposed to have a twin somewhere in the world. Maybe that man is Jed Calhoun's."

Sierra shot her an amused look. "I think that you have Jed Calhoun on the brain."

Suddenly the four other women shifted their gazes

to her. Zoë felt the heat rise in her cheeks. "No, it's not that. I really think this man looks like Jed."

"Right," Natalie said, patting her shoulder. "I found that when I was first besotted with Chance, I saw him everywhere, too. Sounds like you've got it bad, Zoë."

"We've all gone through this," Sophie added. "If you want any advice, just ask one of us."

"I don't—it's not that… I just… I'm not…"

Rad appeared behind Natalie and thankfully interrupted Zoë in midbabble. "Your table is ready, ladies. Right this way."

As they fell in line to follow Rad to the patio, they passed right under the man's table. She didn't glance up, but she felt his gaze on her, and the flame that she'd felt earlier grew hotter. It wasn't until she reached the short flight of stairs that led to the patio that Zoë risked another look at the stranger who reminded her of Jed Calhoun.

He was different from Jed. The dark hair was a bit shorter than the way Jed wore his, and it fell over his forehead. Zoë caught the wink of a diamond on his right pinkie as he lifted his water glass. She couldn't imagine Jed Calhoun ever wearing a pinkie ring. Mr. Elegant had money, she surmised. The glasses also gave him a studious air that Jed Calhoun certainly didn't—

Just then she stumbled, bumped into Sierra and nearly had them both tumbling down the stairs.

"Sorry," she mumbled as she grabbed Sierra's arm and steadied them both. "Good thing I didn't have that second glass of wine."

But it wasn't wine that was making her legs feel so rubbery. It was that man. She was attracted to him. How could she be when for the past two days she'd thought of no one but Jed Calhoun?

JED LET OUT A BREATH he wasn't even aware he'd been holding when he saw Zoë follow Rad and her friends out onto the patio. The last thing he needed right now was a distraction. And Zoë McNamara was definitely that. Just being in the same room with her was affecting him so much that he wasn't keeping his mind on business.

He relaxed his grip on his martini glass, lifted it and took a sip. As he pretended to savor the taste of the British gin he'd requested from the waiter, he let his gaze roam the restaurant. There had to be a reason why Gage hadn't asked Rad to bring him directly to the table.

His old friend was currently moving through the crowd in the bar looking for all the world as if he were searching for someone. Had Gage been followed? By whom? Whoever it was would have to be good because Gage would have taken precautions.

Was Gage merely being cautious? Or was he silently communicating a message? Jed let his own gaze slowly sweep the crowd standing elbow to elbow in the bar area. As Gage finessed his way into one of the seats that Sierra and Zoë had occupied earlier, Jed retraced the path that Gage had woven through the crowd. It wasn't until he'd let his gaze sweep the area for a second time that he spotted her.

Bailey Montgomery was standing at the other end of the bar at the very edge of a group of Georgetown students, and she was deep in conversation with one of them. He'd missed her the first time because she could have passed for an instructor or a grad student in the casual jeans and T-shirt she was wearing. Her hair was loose and she was wearing glasses. It was a thin disguise, but effective. He hadn't spotted her himself, and he should have.

The last time he'd seen her in that alley in Bogotá, she hadn't been wearing the glasses and her hair had been tied back. But her profile was the same, and it would be forever imprinted on his mind. The alley had been illuminated only by a spill of light from a streetlamp. But there had been enough so that he'd seen her silhouetted when she'd turned her head. She'd had her fingers pressed against the pulse in his neck. She'd known that he wasn't dead, not yet at least, and she'd turned to talk to someone else, someone he couldn't see—the marksman who'd pulled the trigger? Was she going to ask for another shot? Her face in profile was the last thing he'd seen before he'd mercifully blacked out.

Jed's mind raced. What was she doing here? He dismissed the coincidence of her just happening to be at the Blue Pepper. Had she followed Gage or had she somehow discovered they were meeting here? And how many people had she brought with her?

The vibration of his cell phone interrupted Jed's thoughts. He reached for it and put it against his ear.

"Change of plans," Gage said.

Thanks to Ryder, Jed knew his cell phone was as secure as technology currently allowed, and he could be pretty sure about Gage's. Obviously, Gage had considered it necessary to risk using this means of communication. For a few seconds, he reviewed his options. A meeting with Gage was out. Bailey knew Gage and she might be watching him. Finally, he said, "Let's try some sleight of hand."

"Listening."

"Put my name on what you brought, pass it to the bartender, and tell him to make sure that it's delivered to Zoë McNamara along with a complimentary bottle of wine. He'll know who she is."

"Okey-dokey," Gage said and disconnected.

Jed continued to hold the cell phone to his ear. One of the things he'd liked most about working with Gage in the past was that he was a man of few words—there'd been no questions, no suggestions. It had been the same on the two missions that they'd worked on together. A man couldn't wish for a better partner than Gage Sinclair. On top of that, Gage had very good eyes. He must have spotted Bailey the moment he'd walked in the door.

But Jed should have spotted Bailey Montgomery himself. All he'd done was feel Zoë's eyes on him. And now he'd drawn her into the picture. Gage's information would be safe with her, and Jed had no doubt that she would get it to him as soon as she could. The problem was would she be safe as long as it was in her possession?

And how long would he have to wait for it? A ripple of frustration moved through him. Keeping his back to the bar, he took another sip of his martini. He waited ten full minutes before he glanced toward the bar again. Gage was glancing at his watch. He'd leave soon. Then it would be Bailey's move. She was still talking to the young man she was standing next to. Would she follow Gage when he left or would she have someone else tail him?

For one long moment, Jed was tempted to walk right up to her and ask her why she'd "killed" him. But this wasn't the time to be impulsive. He'd save that plan for another day.

Tonight, he would enjoy a dinner at the Blue Pepper and wait her out. Before he walked up to Bailey Montgomery, he wanted to know what was in her files.

"A GENTLEMAN AT THE BAR sends this to Zoë McNamara with his compliments." Rad set a bottle of wine on the table and began to distribute glasses.

Zoë stared at the bottle.

"Zoë has a secret admirer," Natalie said. "I'm betting it's Mr. Sexy Glasses."

"Way to go, Zoë," Rory said. Then she leaned closer and whispered. "Sexy underwear will work its magic every time."

"What did he look like?" Zoë asked Rad and then bit

her lip. She wanted Natalie to be right. She wanted it to be the stranger at that table. And that was ridiculous.

"Every lady's dream come true," Rad replied as he poured wine into her glass. "Tall, dark, handsome—"

"Sure sounds like him, Zoë," Natalie commented.

Zoë's heart skipped a little beat, and she could feel the heat rise in her cheeks. What in the world was wrong with her? She didn't want a perfect stranger to be sending her a bottle of wine, especially not that stranger. Not after the way he'd made her feel.

But she couldn't deny that she'd been ogling the man—which was ridiculous. She had let Sierra talk her into a girls' night out with the idea of getting Jed Calhoun out of her mind. Now she couldn't get Mr. Elegant out of her mind. His image had engraved itself on her imagination, that lean body, the strong features. She could recall every detail of his face in profile—the strong chin, straight nose, the warrior's cheekbones. And the glasses.

There was something about him…. If she could just put her finger on it, maybe she could stop thinking about him.

"Did he look like James Bond?" Sierra asked.

Rad filled the last glass. "Which one?"

"Good point. There've been how many?" Sophie asked.

"Five, but who's counting," Rory supplied. "My favorite's Pierce Brosnan."

"You should take Zoë over and introduce her," Sierra said.

"I would, but he left about twenty minutes ago,"

Rad explained. "George was told to hold up the order for a while."

Zoë felt her heart sink. Why should she be feeling a sense of loss because a man she'd never met, never even talked to, had left twenty minutes ago? So what if she'd never gotten to meet him?

Making love with Jed Calhoun was supposed to get her life back on track, not turn her into someone who became irresistibly attracted to strangers. She'd begun to understand exactly what Pandora must have felt when she'd opened that box.

Zoë drew in a deep breath. She was just being ridiculous.

"We're still not sure it was the James Bond man who sent these," Natalie said. Turning to Rad, she continued, "What was the gentleman wearing?"

"It's a good thing we have a cop at the table," Rory said.

"I'm betting an impeccably designed suit and dark framed glasses," Sierra said.

"Oh, you're talking about the Brit," Rad said with a smile. "Sexy accent, Italian shoes, and excellent taste in ties. He bought the one he's wearing at Harrods. They don't make ties like that in the States. And now that I think of it, they really should cast him as the next James Bond."

"Told you so." Sierra gave everyone a smug smile. "Sending a bottle of wine is just the kind of thing 007 would do."

"Oh, the Brit didn't send the wine," Rad said as he placed an envelope in front of Zoë. "It was another man at the bar, and he asked George to see that you got this envelope, too."

Zoë glanced down at the envelope and silently read the name printed neatly in the upper right hand corner.

"What is it?" Sierra asked, leaning closer.

Zoë frowned down at the envelope. "It's not for me. It's for Jed Calhoun."

"Curioser and curioser," Sierra said.

BAILEY MONTGOMERY threaded her way through the couples on the small dance floor, then slipped behind a row of potted palms and pressed herself against the wall. Night had fallen in earnest, and the whole patio was bathed in shadows. Gage Sinclair had given the bartender an envelope and it had been delivered to a table at the far end near the sidewalk. She had to get closer. Sucking in her breath, she squeezed her way past another tree.

She hadn't had any trouble spotting Gage Sinclair. She'd actually felt his presence before she'd picked him out of the crowd. She'd all but forgotten how he'd made her feel all those years ago when he'd been in charge of her training. There'd never been another man that she'd been so intensely aware of.

She'd given it some thought back then, and she'd decided that she couldn't blame her feelings entirely on Gage Sinclair's looks. Oh, he was handsome all right—if you liked your men tall, dark and ruggedly handsome. And she had. Over the years, she'd dated plenty of men who'd fit that description. But they hadn't affected her the way Gage had. The way he evidently still did. She'd been so distracted by him that she'd nearly missed it when he'd handed the envelope to the bartender.

And she was thinking about him now when she should be focusing on that table. Jed Calhoun could be seated there. Keeping close to the wall, she progressed one inch at a time. When she finally reached the last potted palm, she peered through the leaves. There were no men at the table.

Disappointment streamed through her. She shoved it down. Someone at this table was getting a message from Gage Sinclair and she wanted to know who.

The band was playing something with a Latin American beat, and there were couples on the dance floor. Crossing her fingers, Bailey prayed that they would take a break soon. She wanted to hear what the women at the table were saying.

Through the palm leaves, she could just make out the white shape of the envelope. It was sitting on the table in front of the woman at the far end. As Bailey studied her, an odd sense of familiarity moved through her. She'd met the woman before, but where? She never forgot a face. After concentrating on the problem for sixty straight seconds, she let it go. She'd remember sooner or later.

Why had Gage sent the envelope to her? Based on her memories of him, he never did anything without a plan. Therefore, the woman at the far end of the table—whoever she was—was Bailey's ticket to finding Jed Calhoun.

Just then a couple at the table next to the women's rose and started toward the door. Bailey quickly wiggled her way back three trees, stepped out and moved toward the now-vacant table.

As she sat down, she saw the woman at the far end slip the envelope into her bag. A moment later they all stood up and the three tall women on her side of the table momentarily blocked her view. They were chattering about James Bond. Turning, she looked quickly at each one of them, committing the faces to memory. She recognized the tall redhead as a D.C. cop. Natalie Gibbs. Bailey recalled meeting her briefly on a case involving an international art theft ring.

The conversation shifted to movies and whether or not they still had time to take one in. Bailey found herself envying the laughter and the easy camaraderie that these women were enjoying. Working in what was essentially a man's world didn't offer many opportunities for her to hang around with other women.

Bailey checked her thoughts. No wallowing, she scolded herself. For years now, she'd put her career first. As a result, she was very good at what she did. That was important to her.

The cop she'd recognized turned then and Bailey caught another glimpse of the woman at the end of the table. This time something clicked and she remembered exactly who the woman was.

Zoë McNamara was the mousy little analyst who'd been Hadley Richards's protégé during her brief career at the CIA. There'd even been those rumors that she'd had an affair with Hadley before she'd resigned.

What in the world was Gage Sinclair doing using her to deliver a message to Jed Calhoun? Even as she tried to think about the possible implications, the women at the table began to move past her table.

"Welcome to the Blue Pepper. What can I get for you?"

The question from the cheerful waiter only distracted Bailey for a second, but when she glanced back, Zoë McNamara was nowhere to be seen.

8

From his position in the shadows of a store entrance-way across the street, Jed had a fairly good view of the Blue Pepper's patio. Intermittent screens with hanging plants bordered the sidewalk and partially blocked some of the tables from sight, but through a small gap between two screens, he could see Zoë sitting with her friends, and he could just make out her face in the candlelight.

Moments ago he'd seen Rad hand her the envelope from Gage, and she'd put it in her bag. The bad news was that Bailey Montgomery was currently seated with her back to the street at a nearby table. Later, he would berate himself for dragging Zoë into this, but right now, he had to figure out a way to get that envelope.

After he'd left the Blue Pepper, he'd walked around Georgetown, ducked through a few alleys, cut across some lawns and made his way back to the Blue Pepper. In doing so, he'd lost anyone who'd been tailing him, including the men Ryder had assigned to him.

In the twenty minutes or so that he'd been watching her with her friends, he'd had time to examine his motives for having Gage send the envelope to her, and they weren't pure. He'd known that retrieving it would give him an opportunity to see her again. And right now, he could admit to himself that he wanted very much not only to see her again, but to kiss her. To touch her.

He wanted to spend an entire night with Zoë McNamara.

The realization had surprised him. He couldn't recall ever wanting to do that before. In the past, he'd always made sure to keep his relationships with women simple. One way to do that was to lay down ground rules, and number one for him had always been to leave before morning. He'd almost convinced himself that his desire to spend a whole night with Zoë was solely because there'd been so little time and space in that hammock.

For the past thirty minutes, he'd been spinning a little fantasy in which he'd corrected that problem. In his mind, he'd imagined savoring the foreplay they'd hurried through the first time. First, he'd undressed her layer by layer in a bed—a very large bed with cool white sheets and stacks of large, soft pillows. He'd been about to lay her back on those pillows when he'd seen Bailey Montgomery sit down at a table near Zoë's.

The reality check was sudden and abrupt, sending all the very enjoyable images he'd conjured up right out of his mind and leaving a cold knot in his stomach. Obviously, Agent Montgomery had seen Gage pass the envelope to the bartender and she'd waited to identify the recipient.

Jed's mind raced. In another few minutes, Zoë, Sierra and their friends would leave, and Bailey Montgomery would follow Zoë. The woman was good at her job. She might even approach Zoë and try to talk her out of the envelope. At the very least, she would have Zoë watched and followed.

He had to get the information Gage was sending him before that happened. But how? Through the gap in the screens, he saw Zoë rise from the chair. She was getting ready to leave. He strode forward out of the shop entranceway and crossed the street. As he reached the curb, Zoë glanced his way and their eyes met. He felt the power of the connection like a punch in his stomach. For a second, it stopped him in his tracks. No other woman had ever affected him this way. Only Zoë. Gathering himself, he moved quickly and quietly toward her.

ZOË BLINKED, but the man didn't disappear. He wasn't an image she'd conjured up in her mind. He'd come back. And he was walking toward the restaurant with that same purposeful stride that she'd noticed earlier. A thrill of excitement moved through her. In the glow of the streetlights, he looked more dangerous than ever.

Through the small gap in between two screens, she tracked his progress as he stepped up on the sidewalk. Had he come back for her? Another little thrill streamed through her.

No, of course he hadn't. What was she thinking? Being swept away by a mysterious stranger was just a popular fantasy—a very popular one with women, according to her research. She'd never quite understood it herself. After all, the days of pirates and highwaymen were over. And surely, no one wanted them back. No woman wanted to be swept away by a total stranger in real life. Did she?

As he drew closer, Zoë realized that a very real part of her *did* want that to happen. Now that she'd indulged in her more passionate side, she seemed to be having a little trouble controlling it.

She wanted to run, but she wasn't sure if she wanted to run toward this man or away. Not that it mattered, because she couldn't move. She could barely breathe. Her heart was pounding so hard that it was blocking out all other sounds, and all of her senses were heightened.

Out of the corner of her eye, she could see that the Gibbs sisters were engaged in a lively conversation. The discussion about whether or not they should take in a movie before they called it a night seemed faint and far away. No one was paying any attention to her. And why should they? She'd barely contributed anything to their conversations all evening.

She'd been too busy thinking about this man and the magnetic pull he seemed to have on her. Was this her payback for giving in to desire and making love with Jed Calhoun? Was she going to feel this way about every man she met? But it wasn't every man who affected her this way.

Just this one and Jed Calhoun. Even the fascination she'd had with Lucifer for six months paled in comparison.

Though the other women couldn't see him behind the screen, he was close enough that she could almost touch him. And she was shocked by the greed she felt rising in her to do just that. In the dim light, his face was shadowed, but she could feel his eyes on her, and she could imagine him touching her. An arrow of heat pierced her, and her hand rose and reached—

"Zoë, we have to talk."

He spoke so softly that Zoë wasn't sure she caught the words. Then he was striding soundlessly toward the corner. Loss streamed through her in the same way that it had when Rad had told her the Brit had left.

No. Zoë drew in a breath and lifted her chin. She wouldn't let him walk away again. This time she'd follow him. She had to discover why he had this effect on her.

A quick look around assured her that no one was paying any attention to her. Glancing back through the gap in the screens, she could see that the Brit was already turning the corner. Saying goodbye to Sierra and the other women would only waste precious minutes, so Zoë squeezed between two screens and raced after him. It was only as she reached the corner and saw that he was nearly a block ahead of her that it struck her.

The mysterious stranger she was following into the night had known her name.

JED RISKED ONE LOOK BACK as he turned the corner. Relief flooded through him when he saw that she was following him. Thank heavens. In spite of his disguise, she must have recognized him in the same way that he'd known on some level whose eyes had been on him in the Blue Pepper.

Still, he didn't slow his pace. Because he couldn't discount the very real possibility that Bailey Montgomery or someone she may have stationed outside the restaurant was even now following Zoë, he wanted to put some distance between them and the restaurant.

They had some time, he figured. He was pretty sure that no one had seen him pause to talk to Zoë. From a distance, it would have appeared that he'd merely stopped to look over the restaurant, perhaps checking for empty tables. And Zoë had been quick to follow. At the end of the second block, he turned left onto a residential street and then slipped into the shadow of a tall hedge and waited.

The street was quiet. Leaves rustled overhead, and a short distance away a dog barked. A dark-colored SUV pulled around the corner and then speeded up. Halfway down the block, it turned into a driveway.

Jed heard her footsteps, and that was all it took to have him turning and his whole body tightening. He swore at himself silently. This was not the time for indulging in fantasies. He was here to get the envelope and to get Zoë safely home. How much should he tell her? That was what he should be concentrating on.

The less she knew the better. He'd already involved her too deeply in his problems.

The moment that she came into view, he spoke in a whisper. "Zoë, over here."

She started, then turned and walked toward him, stopping when she was just out of his reach. He found he had to put some effort into not closing the distance between them.

"First, I'm warning you that I'm a black belt in karate. So don't try anything."

Surprise shot through him, and for a moment he couldn't think of anything to say. It was the second time that Zoë McNamara had rendered him speechless. Was that why she fascinated him so darn much? Jed studied her for a moment, while she studied him right back.

Her flat but carefully worded warning, along with the determined look in her eyes told him that she definitely hadn't recognized him. Yet she'd followed him into the night. The realization gave him an odd and very exciting thrill.

"Okay. I won't try anything." He used the same British accent he'd used in the restaurant. "If that's first, what's second?"

She lifted her chin and met his eyes steadily. "How did you know my name?"

This was his chance, Jed thought, to tell her who he was. Instead, he said, "I asked the maître d'."

"Oh." Her eyes widened, in surprise, he thought. But

she recovered quickly. "Who are you and why did you ask me to follow you?"

He should tell her now. But once again, he ignored the opportunity.

"Well?" She crossed her arms in front of her, and he could hear the soft sound of her foot tapping.

He very nearly had to smile. She was just so damn cute. Then the moonlight suddenly shifted on her skin, and he became very aware of just how much it reminded him of fine porcelain. But it wouldn't feel anything like cool, hard porcelain. He badly wanted to draw a finger along that lifted chin and feel the mix of warmth and softness and strength.

Her brows lifted. "I'm waiting."

For a moment, Jed said nothing. This was where he should simply tell her who he was, ask for the envelope and take her home. But in the moonlight, he could only think of doing one thing. It wasn't rational, but the desire to kiss her again, taste her again, possess her again had been growing ever since he'd turned and realized that she was there in the Blue Pepper watching him. In spite of his promise to himself not to go near her again, and in spite of the possible danger right now, he wanted to prolong the moment. He wanted her here with him.

"I'm Ethan Blair, and I asked you to follow me because I want to kiss you."

She blinked first and then swallowed. In the silence that stretched between them, he noticed the way the pulse at the base of her throat had quickened.

"If you don't want me to kiss you, you'd better say so now." Unable to prevent himself, he put his hands on her arms and drew her closer.

She lifted one hand to his chest and he stilled. "It's not that. Because I do want you to kiss me. Very much."

When he tried to draw her closer, she pressed harder against his chest.

"I'm just trying to understand it. I don't know you from Adam," she said with a frown. "And I'm sort of involved with another man."

"Sort of?" he asked.

"It's complicated. But I'm not sure I've given up on the idea of pursuing something more with him."

A mix of feelings streamed through him. She was talking about him. He was sure of it. Once again, he passed up his chance to tell her who he really was.

"So why did you follow me if you're sort of involved with this other man?" he asked.

Her frown deepened. "Because from the moment I saw you sitting at that table, I felt this…connection. And desire."

He drew her closer, but she pressed her hand more firmly against his chest.

"You're playing with fire to tell me something like that and then try to push me away."

"You remind me of him…in a way," she said.

"So you followed me because you want this other man?" He wasn't quite sure how he felt about that.

"I told you it was complicated. I also followed you

because," She shifted on her feet and said more softly, "I want to know why you can have this effect on me."

Jed did pull her closer then, and this time she didn't resist. "Maybe you don't have to figure it out." He drew her up onto her toes until he could wrap one arm around her and press her body to his in that perfect fit he remembered. Then he rubbed his thumb over her bottom lip. "Maybe you should just enjoy it."

"I…I can't think when you do that."

"Good," he murmured as he brushed his lips against hers. "That means I'm doing something right."

"But—"

He traced her bottom lip with his tongue.

"I—"

"Shh." In some part of his mind, he knew that if he were thinking straight, he wouldn't be kissing her as Ethan Blair. And he certainly shouldn't be doing it on a Georgetown street. Then he pressed his mouth more firmly to hers and tumbled them both into the kiss.

Sensations shot through him—everything he remembered, and more. Her taste was hot and sweet. Only it was more intense than he remembered it. And the heat shot up as if the time they'd spent apart had only stoked the fire.

Each little explosion of pleasure was sharper than he'd remembered. Her teeth nipped his bottom lip and shot a bolt of desire through him. Her hands gripped his shoulders, and he felt the pressure of her nails through the material of the thin fabric. He moved his hand in one smooth sweep up her side and then covered her breast. Then he changed the angle of the kiss. The need he tasted was so intense, so desperate, and such a perfect match to his own. He could have sworn that the ground under his feet had shifted.

Then he felt the sharp jolt of something pressing into his back, and Zoë was yanked from his grasp.

"Don't make any sudden moves, and we won't have to hurt you," a gruff voice behind him said.

ZOË 'S HEAD WAS SPINNING, but the sharp spurt of pure adrenaline helped her to focus. Several things were crystal clear. The huge mountain of a man who was currently holding her arm in a viselike grip had jerked her from Ethan Blair's arms, and he now had the barrel of a gun pressed into her temple. Another man, shorter, leaner and much meaner looking, was standing behind Ethan, and though she couldn't see it, she strongly suspected that he had a gun, too.

"I'll cooperate fully if you'll let the lady go." Ethan's tone was soft, the accent clipped.

The man gave a soft laugh, and the sound made Zoë's skin go icy. "It's the little lady we came for," he said. "If you don't want a bullet in your spine, you'll do what you're told."

The beefy man next to her pressed the gun more firmly against her temple, and Zoë found that she was having trouble breathing. Adrenaline was keeping at least a part of her mind sharp, but the fear lodged in her throat was blocking her windpipe. She concentrated on getting some oxygen into her system.

"Now, we're going to walk up the street to that SUV."

Zoë spotted it parked in a driveway four houses up the block. The motor was idling.

"We'll go first," the man said to Ethan. "Two by two, just as if we're taking a little nighttime stroll. No false moves or Bobby will put a bullet in the little lady, and we wouldn't want that."

Zoë and the linebacker fell into step behind Ethan and the other man. They must have looked like an odd kind of a parade. The thought had a bubble of laughter rising, and there was a strange ringing in her ears—a combination of hysteria and panic, no doubt.

Think, Zoë told herself. *Think.* She made herself take in another breath. The one thing that had been stressed in her karate classes was never give the opponent an advantage. So they couldn't get into that car. Bobby and his buddy didn't want to shoot them in the middle of a Georgetown street. So the best chance of escape for her and Ethan was right now.

Zoë focused on her surroundings. Bobby had a firm grip on her arm, but she was banking on the fact that since she hadn't once struggled, she'd lured him into complacency. Plus, he probably figured he could handle anything she could try.

What was she going to try? That was the question. They were quickly closing the distance to the dark SUV. Two more driveways to go. Out of the corner of her eye she caught movement as a man stepped out of the front door of a Federal-style house. He was followed by a sizable dog. It was too dark for her to recognize the breed, but Zoë prayed it was vicious. A golden retriever was not going to be of much help. Then relying on pure instinct, she stumbled and let out a startled cry.

"What the—" The man with Ethan turned his head.

Noting that her head was currently beneath the muzzle of Bobby's gun, Zoë used all her strength to bring her left foot down hard on his instep.

Bobby grunted, tightening his grip on her arm, but she still managed to bring her knee up hard into his crotch.

His howl had the man across the street, yelling, "Hey, what's going on?"

The dog started barking.

"Help!" Zoë shrieked. She broke free of Bobby's grip just as Ethan placed a well-aimed kick in the face of his captor.

Before she had time to do much more than register the skill involved in the move, he grabbed her hand and muttered, "Run."

Run they did. They'd only taken a few steps before she heard a muffled sound and Ethan stumbled, almost causing them both to go down. But at the last moment, she caught her balance and pulled him forward. His legs were longer than hers, and since she had to run three steps to his two, it was difficult to get into a rhythm. As they turned the first corner, she glanced back to see that the SUV was backing out of the driveway.

Once back on a commercial street, Ethan dragged her into a shop entranceway and they flattened themselves against a glass window. Through it Zoë saw the black SUV turn the corner and drive slowly past. Fifteen long seconds ticked by before Ethan said, "They turned right. They're probably going to drive around widening their circle until they spot us."

Then grabbing her hand, he pulled her out onto the sidewalk and they ran in the same direction. As they stormed up the next block, hand in hand, Zoë worked to get into a rhythm. Ethan stopped at the corner and shoved her behind him long enough to send his gaze up and down the cross street.

"Clear," was all he said. Then he dragged her diagonally across the intersection. A block later, he pulled her across the street and urged her down a flight of steps. Tourists were familiar with the stairs because they'd figured in a prominent scene in the movie *The Exorcist*. A body had been found at the bottom. As they hit the spot running, Zoë tried not to think about the body.

At the next corner, Ethan didn't stop, didn't even slow his pace. They simply ran around it and raced on. Later, she would recall how surreal it was—the bursts of muffled laughter that floated out from pubs and restaurants, the odd stares they received from the few pedestrians they zigged and zagged around, the patches of streetlamp light that they raced in and out of.

Her calves and lungs had begun to burn by the time she realized they'd left the commercial area and entered what appeared to be a winding drive through a park. When a car turned the corner ahead of them, Ethan jerked her behind a large elm and pressed her against the trunk.

Zoë concentrated on getting her breath. Her lungs were on fire. But it wasn't just her lungs that were burning up. Her body seemed to be on fire at each and every contact point it made with Ethan Blair's. Somewhere in the back of her mind, she heard the car make its way slowly up the drive. But even as the sound of the motor faded in the distance, Ethan didn't move.

She didn't want him to.

The realization should have shocked her. Someone had tried to kidnap them, and they were running for their lives. She should be thinking about that. But she couldn't seem to focus on the danger they were in. Not when her eyes were staring at the pulse that was beating in his throat. She wanted to put her lips against that pulse. She wanted to taste his skin. At the thought, the heat she was feeling grew more intense and her own pulse raced even faster. Her gaze moved to his mouth. She wanted to kiss him again.

The one kiss that they'd shared hadn't been like most first kisses. He hadn't taken the time to tempt or explore. Instead, he'd taken instant possession of her mouth as if they'd kissed before.

But they hadn't. She would have remembered the slow way he'd probed her mouth with his tongue as if he'd been determined to sample and savor every part of it. Just thinking about it had that strange ache building inside of her, just as it had in the shadow of that hedge.

When she felt his finger move lightly along the underside of her jaw, she began to tremble. He tipped her face up so that she had to meet his eyes. For a long moment, she didn't move, didn't speak as a longing filled her. She was almost sure she saw a reflection of what she was feeling in his eyes.

"You're really something," he said as he dragged the pad of his thumb along her bottom lip.

The heat inside of her grew so intense that she thought some of it must be escaping as steam.

Then, with a sigh, Ethan drew back from her. "We can't stay here."

She hadn't even realized that she had grabbed fistfuls of his jacket to keep him close until he pried her fingers loose.

Disappointment and embarrassment streamed through her. But he was right. Of course, they couldn't stay here—wherever that was. They weren't out of danger yet. And they were in a public place.

She dragged her gaze away from his and tried to gather her thoughts. And that's when she saw it—a dark stain on the sleeve of his jacket, just above where she'd grabbed it.

"You're bleeding." Some of the blood was on her hand. Even in the pale light from the streetlamp, it looked bright red. "They shot you."

"So they did. They must have used a silencer." With

a finger under her chin, he urged her gaze upward until it met his. "It's just a scratch, Zoë."

"They could have killed you," she said.

"You were the one they were after. Why?"

9

IT HAD BEEN SEVEN YEARS since Gage Sinclair had engaged in any cloak-and-dagger work for his country, and he had to admit that doing a favor for Jed Calhoun had brought back a thrill he'd been missing. Most of the consulting work he did was analytical and it didn't shoot the same zing through the blood as the kind of jobs he'd done before his injury.

He glanced at the digital clock on the dashboard of his car and then back up at the windows in Zoë McNamara's apartment. In the last ten minutes, since Bailey Montgomery had entered through the front door, he hadn't seen so much as a flicker of light.

She was good. Gage Sinclair frowned as he thought about that. When Jed had faxed him the information two days ago that Bailey Montgomery had been the one who'd shot him in Bogotá, Gage had been surprised. That she'd failed in her mission had surprised him even more.

Somehow she'd learned that he was going to meet Jed Calhoun at the Blue Pepper tonight. That meant that either his phone or Jed's had been tapped. It also meant that Jed was probably right and Bailey had spotted him at that party.

He intended to check his phones. In the meantime, he wanted very much to know what Agent Montgomery was up to.

He'd found himself a spot across the street from the Blue Pepper after he'd left the envelope with the bartender. When Bailey hadn't followed him, he'd known that she was sticking around to see where the envelope ended up. That's what he would have done.

He'd watched "Ethan Blair" leave and return and then leave again with Zoë following. Believing that Jed had that end of things under control, he'd remained to keep an eye on Bailey, and he'd followed her to Zoë's apartment.

It had taken her less than twenty minutes to get a name and an address for Zoë McNamara. Pretty slick work. But then Bailey Montgomery was the best agent he'd ever recruited and trained.

And she was still very easy on the eyes. All in all, she was one well-put-together package. Not only was she beautiful in a classic sense, but she'd been first in her class at Yale when he'd met her. Over the years, he'd kept tabs on her career, and he couldn't think of one other assignment she hadn't successfully completed.

Truth was, he'd kept his eye on Bailey Montgomery over the years because in the early days he'd had a yen for her. Of course, he'd never acted on it. Number one, he was her senior by eight years, and fraternizing with fellow agents was frowned upon. Plus he'd been her mentor. And while he might have been tempted to ignore all that after she'd been at the agency for a while, Bailey Montgomery wouldn't have. She was a stickler for following rules. One of the reasons he'd gone back into fieldwork was to get away from a growing attraction that he couldn't act on.

Later, after he'd left the CIA, there'd been other reasons why he hadn't acted on his attraction to her, not the least of which was the fact that he'd lost a leg during his last little government caper. It had taken a while, but modern medicine worked miracles, and there were very few people who were aware that he wore a prosthesis.

Gage's eyes narrowed as Bailey reappeared out of the shadows at the side of Zoë's house, then walked quickly down the street to her black Beetle convertible. In Gage's mind the car suited her to a tee—the color was conservative but the style was wasn't.

Maybe that was what had always intrigued him about Bailey Montgomery—the fact that she was prim and proper on the outside, but there was that hint of the risk taker underneath.

Case in point: Miss Follow-the-Rules had just broken into Zoë McNamara's apartment. He couldn't help but wonder what other rules she might be willing to break.

And then there was the big question. What had caused her to bungle what should have been a fairly simple job in that alley in Bogotá?

He intended to find the answers.

JED PACED BACK AND FORTH in his hotel suite as he waited for the front desk to pick up. A glance at Zoë, sitting a few feet away on a sofa, assured him that some color had come back into her cheeks. She'd been a bit pale when he'd bundled her into the taxi. But she'd certainly kept her cool when those two men had grabbed them.

He'd barely felt the bullet, he'd been so focused on getting her away from those men. But his blood had been on a slow boil since he'd gotten her safely inside the room. Before that, he'd had to keep his mind clear and sharp.

That's what he should have done when he'd been in the shadow of that hedge kissing her. If he hadn't been so lost in that kiss, in her, he would have known that someone was approaching. He'd nearly gotten them both killed. He would have if she hadn't come to the rescue.

His safest option had been to bring her here to his hotel suite. He certainly couldn't have taken her to her apartment, not when there was a good chance that whoever had sent those two thugs had identified her.

His hunch was that Bailey Montgomery had sent the two men. It made sense that she would have come with backup. She'd seen the waiter deliver Gage's envelope to Zoë, and she must have ordered the two men to snatch Zoë.

Thanks to him, Zoë was now in mortal danger.

"Front desk," said a voice in his ear.

"Room 549. I want you to send up a first aid kit as soon as possible."

"Are you injured, sir?"

"No." He'd been lucky. The bullet had only grazed his flesh. He'd rinsed the wound in the bathroom and tied a hand towel around it as a temporary bandage. He'd also called Ryder on his cell phone, told him what had happened and insisted that Ryder send men to protect Zoë.

"Sir, we have a policy. We have to note down the reason whenever a first aid kit is requested."

Jed called on his sorely depleted store of patience. "On our walk back from dinner, my wife took a little spill and scraped her knee."

"Did she fall on the hotel grounds?"

Jed heard real concern in the desk clerk's voice, probably not because a guest had sustained an injury but because of possible litigation. "No, we were in Georgetown when she fell. I just want to make sure it doesn't get infected."

"I'll send it up right away, sir. Will there be anything else?"

"A bottle of brandy." They both could use some. "What do you have?"

"I'll connect you to room service. They'll be able to help you."

While he listened to another phone ring, Jed returned his gaze to Zoë. He hadn't been able to take his eyes off of her for very long since they'd gotten here. He should never have asked Gage to send that envelope to her.

She had such a pull on him. No other woman had ever affected him this way. Even now, he couldn't look at her without being very aware that there was a bed through the open door to his left—a bed that had been carefully turned down for the night.

Studying her, he was aware once again of the difference in the way she was dressed tonight. The lace and silk top he'd noticed in the Blue Pepper was the sexiest thing he'd ever seen her wear. And he couldn't help wondering if she was wearing anything beneath those jeans.

Ruthlessly, he shoved the thought away. He had to decide how to answer the questions she was sure to ask as soon as he hung up the phone.

He knew that she was even now formulating and categorizing them in her mind. She'd start with the one he hadn't fully answered before he'd kissed her.

"Who are you?"

That was the question all right. If he told her the truth, that he was Jed Calhoun, she'd want to know why he was disguised, and he'd have to tell her his story— that he was supposed to be dead, and that if he showed up alive, he'd have to face murder charges.

She'd keep his secret. He didn't doubt that for a minute. What was holding him back was the fact that if she knew the truth, she might be in even more danger than she was now.

There wasn't a doubt in his mind that Bailey Montgomery would track her down. Ryder could protect her from the thugs in the SUV, but if Agent Montgomery questioned her, it might be better if Zoë didn't know any more than that she'd met a man named Jed Calhoun who'd been living with his friend Ryder Kane on a house-boat. And that Jed Calhoun had completely disappeared.

"Room service," a voice said in his ear.

"I want a bottle of your best brandy and two glasses," Jed said.

"Let me see what we have available."

"Whatever you have will do." But Jed realized that he'd been put on hold.

He shifted his gaze back to Zoë. If he remained Ethan Blair, then he could insist that she remain here for the night. He could sleep on the pullout sofa and drive her home in the morning where Ryder would have two men watching her.

Still pacing, he turned that scenario over in his mind.

Just then, the voice on the other end of the line rattled off the names of three brandies. Jed chose one and listened while the man repeated it and confirmed the room number.

As he hung up the phone, Zoë rose from the settee. For a moment neither of them said a thing. In spite of his resolve, Jed wanted nothing more than to go to her and finish the kiss he'd started earlier.

"Is your arm all right?" she said.

Jed very nearly smiled. Not who are you or who were those men and why did they want to kill us. Instead, she was still concerned about his arm. Sooner or later, he was going to figure out why she could always surprise him.

"You handled yourself very well back there," he said.

"So did you. I imagine you do this a lot, don't you?"

His brows shot up. "You mean get shot?"

"No, I mean escape from goons like that. You knew what you were doing. You reminded one of my friends at the Blue Pepper of James Bond, and I think she might have been right."

"James Bond would never have gotten you in a scrape like that. You saved both of our lives. All in all, I'd say you'd make a pretty good Bond girl."

ZOË FELT THE HEAT rise in her cheeks. If the edge of the sofa hadn't been pressing into the backs of her legs, she would have retreated a step. For the past five minutes while he'd been on the phone, she'd been staring out the window so that she wouldn't sit there gawking at him.

When he'd been cleaning his wound in the bathroom, he'd unbuttoned his shirt and torn the sleeve off, and the moment he'd stepped back into the living area of the suite, she'd caught herself staring at the exposed skin. And fantasizing. The strength of her desire to run her hands over that skin had shocked her.

Now he was standing only a few feet away, and she was staring again. At his throat. She didn't just want to touch. She wanted to taste him, too.

"So you have a black belt in karate," he said.

She moistened her lips and dragged her mind back to what she wanted to say. "I've never before tried any of the moves outside of class. And I wasn't sure if I'd get the chance to use any of them. I…" she twisted her hands together. "It was that man and his dog who saved us. We were lucky."

He reached out and stroked a lock of her hair with his fingers. "I was lucky."

Zoë couldn't feel her knees anymore. Every time he touched her, she melted. Jed Calhoun had been the only man who'd ever affected her that way. Now Ethan could do that to her, too. Was there a whole slew of other men out there who could make her feel this way? The thought made her shiver.

"You're cold," Jed said.

"Yes…no." Before she could babble further, there was a knock at the door.

Jed glanced at his watch. "That was quick." For a moment he looked as if he was as reluctant to walk away as she was for him do that. Then he turned and moved to the door of the suite.

Zoë drew in a deep breath, but she wasn't sure whether what she was feeling was relief or disappointment. While he checked the peephole then handled the waiter, she tried to gather her thoughts. But she couldn't seem to think straight as long as he was in the same room with her.

When he came back, he was carrying a small first aid kit and two snifters of brandy. He pressed one of them into her hands. "Take a sip," he ordered. "I think we both need it."

Zoë was only too willing to take a taste. She was sure

she needed something, and for now, she welcomed the warmth that spread through her. She had to get a grip.

He took a seat on the other side of the coffee table. She watched as he opened the first aid kit and removed the towel from his arm. The mark that the bullet had left was angry looking, but it had stopped bleeding. She couldn't take her eyes off of him as he swabbed the wound with antiseptic and pressed a gauze pad against it. Hunger built inside of her again.

When he fumbled with the tape, she set down her glass and moved around the table to sit next to him on the sofa. "Let me help."

Taking the tape from him, she pressed it against the gauze and then smoothed it over his upper arm. His skin was warm beneath her fingers, and she felt the hardness of the muscles beneath. This close, she could smell him. The scent of the soap he'd used to clean the wound mixed with the pungent odor of the antiseptic and something else that she suspected was unique to him, yet somehow familiar. The hunger that had been building inside of her spiked.

Her hands trembled as she cut off another piece of tape and repeated the procedure. This time, her fingers lingered on his skin.

In just a minute she would move away, she promised herself. But as seconds ticked by, she couldn't seem to get control of the battle going on inside of her.

Less than two days ago, she'd experienced these same feelings for another man. But Jed Calhoun was

gone. Ethan Blair was here. And she didn't want to take
her hands off of him. She wanted to move her hands up
and over his shoulders. No, more than that, she wanted
to touch him everywhere.

Before she could follow through on her desire, Ethan
took her hands in his and raised one of them to his lips.
His mouth brushed her fingers, his breath whispered
over her knuckles, and the intensity of the sensations
made her tremble again.

"You're so responsive," he murmured as he lowered
her hands.

Her gaze flew to his then, and the breath caught in
her throat. His face was so close. She knew it was a
mistake to stay this way even for a moment. She should
pull her hands from his and stand up, go back to her seat
on the other sofa.

But she didn't move. She was aware of heat without
being quite sure if it came from him or her. It was
melting her bones. His eyes were so blue—the way
she'd always imagined Lucifer's to be. That was the last
errant thought that tumbled into her mind before her
brain simply shut down.

It was the most natural thing in the world to put her
hand on the back of his neck and draw his mouth to hers.
Instantly, she felt the same heat, the same rush of power,
the same sharp needs she'd felt before. This was what
she wanted, everything she wanted.

10

HE'D WANTED THIS, needed this. Dragging his mouth from hers, Ethan took it on a quick, desperate journey down her throat. Her scent swam in his head, her flavors flooded his mouth. And still greed built inside of him. He couldn't get enough. He might never get enough.

Unable to stop himself, he brought his mouth back to hers and plundered. No other woman had ever made him feel this way. Weak, winded. He could feel his control draining as if someone had pulled a plug. He nipped her bottom lip and heard her quick, quiet moan. Images cartwheeled through his mind. The bed was only a few yards away. He could have her there, naked and beneath him, in a matter of seconds.

Then he heard his cell phone ring. It was barely more than an irritating buzz, like the sound of a mosquito circling near his ear. But it rang again. And again. One thought managed to penetrate the haze that had settled like a thick blanket over his brain.

Ryder had news about the SUV. Jed had called his buddy as he and Zoë had made their way to the hotel.

It took all his strength to draw away and set Zoë back against the cushions of the sofa. Fumbling for his cell in his pocket, he rose and moved away from her.

"Yeah?"

"You okay?" Ryder asked.

For the first time in his life, Jed realized that he wasn't sure about that. "Fine," he said.

"My men have been cruising around the streets in the vicinity of the Blue Pepper, but they didn't spot the SUV. Those goons must have given up trying to find you."

"It was a long shot," Jed said.

"Been nice if it had paid off."

The fact that it hadn't meant they weren't any closer to finding out who'd sent those two men. Probably Bailey Montgomery, but it would have been nice to be sure.

"I've got two of my men in the lobby of your hotel," Ryder continued. "Try not to give them the slip, this time."

"Yeah," Jed said.

"And there are another two at Zoë's apartment who'll take over once she returns there."

"I want them to stick close."

"Like flypaper," Ryder promised before he cut the connection.

Jed didn't look at Zoë, not until he'd taken a seat on the sofa across from hers and indulged in a swallow of brandy. Then he met her eyes. "It would be better if we didn't kiss again."

She said nothing. But he saw something in those huge eyes of hers. Hurt?

"It's not that I don't want to. You must know that I do. But…it's complicated. I never should have asked you to follow me tonight. I nearly got you killed."

"You are some kind of a secret agent, aren't you? And those men were after you?"

He'd evaded her implied question when she mentioned James Bond, but he was going to have to tell her something. "I've done some contract work for the government," he said carefully.

"I knew it." There was excitement and curiosity in her eyes now.

"The important thing is that you may still be in danger," he said. "That was the friend of mine that I called on the way to the hotel. He's going to have two men watch you. Those thugs were after you."

"I can't understand why. But I was thinking while you were in the bathroom. A few days ago when I was driving out near the Chesapeake, getting lost, there was an SUV, very similar to that one tonight, and I thought it might be following me. But I'm sure it was just a co-incidence. I can't imagine why anyone would be interested in me."

Jed studied her for a moment. He didn't believe in coincidences. He recalled his gut feeling that someone had followed him the night of Sierra and Ryder's engagement party. He hadn't gotten a good look at the vehicle, but it could have been an SUV. When Zoë saw it, could it have been prowling the roads trying to find the location of Ryder's houseboat? Or had it been following her?

"At any rate, you shouldn't blame yourself for what happened tonight." She paused, then added, "I might have followed you even if you hadn't asked."

Jed stared at her. She shouldn't be able to thrill him by saying something like that. She shouldn't be able to make him ache with need just by sitting there, looking at him. But he couldn't prevent himself from asking, "Why would you have followed me? I'm a stranger."

"I told you before. I felt this connection from the first minute our eyes met," she said, looking slightly uncomfortable with her admission.

He forced himself to lean back against the sofa cushions. He willed his muscles to relax. "I felt the same thing."

"Really?" She leaned forward. "Does it happen to you often?"

"No. There's only been one woman who's affected me this way. You."

"Oh." Her hand trembled again, and she set the snifter down on the table with an audible click. "I see."

"How about you? Does this instant attraction happen to you often?" he asked.

Zoë folded her hands together in her lap. "Only twice. With you and that one other man."

"The one you mentioned before, the one you were involved with?"

"Yes. But even with him, I didn't ask him to kiss me the first time we met."

Another thrill moved through him. She had to be

talking about him. But he had to know. "What's this other man like?"

She frowned a little in an expression he'd learned was habitual when she was thinking. "You're very like him in height and weight. There's even a strong resemblance in your facial features especially in the line of your jaw. Coloring and body language aside, you could probably pass for brothers. But beneath the surface, you're very different."

"Different how?" Jed asked. He was curious now and a little amused that he was quizzing her about his competition—which was himself.

"He's very laid-back, but I think that's partially a facade. He reminds me of a big jungle cat sleeping in the sun. He looks lazy and harmless enough, but I have a feeling he can be fast and lethal when he wants to. Do you know what I mean?"

He nodded. He knew exactly what she meant, and he was impressed that she'd seen him that clearly.

"He also tends to view life through a—" she paused to search for a word "—lens of irony. That makes him seem cynical at times."

Jed Calhoun to a tee, he thought. "And how do you see me?"

"I haven't known you as long. But I sense that you're much more serious. You're smoother, more sophisticated and very intense. One of my friends at the Blue Pepper thinks you're a prime candidate to become the next James Bond."

His smile was wry. "Hardly. And this other man, does he remind you of James Bond?"

After a moment, Zoë shook her head. "He's a little harder to categorize."

Jed wasn't sure how he felt about that description.

"There's a hint of danger there, but other than that he's not really like you at all."

"And yet you were very attracted to him?"

"Yes."

An odd mix of pleasure and something else moved through him. Was it jealousy he was feeling because she'd been attracted to him both as himself and disguised as Ethan Blair? That was ridiculous.

But the words were out before he could prevent them. "Are you attracted to me just as much as you were to this other man?"

"Yes."

One word. Just that one word had all of his earlier resolutions—not to kiss her again, to sleep on one of the sofas—disappearing like vapors. There would be a price to pay for this. But he'd gladly pay it.

He rose and went to her, took her hands and drew her up off the sofa. Jed had never given her much in the way of words. So this time he'd be the one to ask. "Zoë, would you let me make love to you?"

ZOË DIDN'T THINK she could have wanted him any more, but his words and even more, the look in his eyes, turned the desire she'd been feeling into a burning ache. Hadn't she wanted him to say those words, willed him to say them, since they'd first kissed?

"There's one thing you should understand. After tonight, we'll never see each other again," he said. "I'm almost certain that those men were after you because of me. In order to keep you safe, I won't be able to have any further contact with you. Knowing that, will you make love with me just this once?"

Just this once. The words played themselves over in her mind. It had only been once with Jed Calhoun. It would only be once with Ethan Blair. But she wasn't going to say no. Tomorrow there'd be time enough to analyze why she might be attracting men who couldn't, or wouldn't, stick around. She'd leave that for the psychologist in her. Tonight she was just going to indulge in her wild side again.

She smiled at him. "I thought you'd never ask."

JED TOOK HER HAND, raised it to his mouth and brushed his lips across her knuckles. Making love to her might not be wise, but the harm would be minimal, wouldn't it? They'd spend one night together as Ethan Blair and Zoë McNamara. In the morning he'd get up before she woke, he'd take the envelope that she'd stuffed into her bag, and he'd leave her in the care of the two men who were down in the lobby.

Turning her hand over, he pressed a kiss into her palm and savored the way her eyes darkened. This time, both Jed Calhoun and Ethan Blair would stay the hell away from her until the danger was over. Then, because he could no longer prevent himself, he framed her face with his hands and covered her mouth with his.

Oh, yes, this was what it had felt like the last time he'd kissed her—this giant leap off a very steep cliff. Desire built at such a breakneck speed that he thought of dragging her to the floor and taking her there before either of them could change their minds. When he finally drew back to think, to breathe, she said his name, "Ethan…"

A series of little alarm bells went off in the back of his mind. He was making love to her as Ethan this time, and not Jed. He'd better remember that. If Jed had given her fun, Ethan, his more serious counterpart, would make an attempt at giving her romance. Taking her hand he drew her with him into the bedroom.

Moonlight streamed into the room, splashing across the bed. He purposely didn't switch on the lights. Turning to her, he touched only her hair. He'd been wanting to over and over again since he'd noticed in the bar that she was wearing it down. When he rubbed it between his fingers, he caught the scent of vanilla.

Jed went with his instincts, so Ethan would have a plan. He drew a finger along the edge of the lace camisole that she was wearing, absorbing the softness of the fabric and the even softer skin that lay beneath it. He'd been wanting to do that all evening, too.

Jed had asked her to strip, so Ethan would undress her. After undoing the button, he slipped the jacket off her shoulders and let it fall to the floor. Jed had asked her to take a tumble with him in a hammock, so Ethan would make love to her slowly just as he'd been about to do in his fantasy.

He slipped his fingers beneath the camisole and drew it slowly over her head. And that was when his plan began to fade. She wasn't wearing a bra.

Surprise and delight shot through him. "Zoë," he murmured as he slid his hands from her waist to just under her arms. Then he lightly brushed the pads of his thumbs over her nipples. They were already erect and hard.

So was he. Every muscle in his body had tightened in response. A pulse was beating at her throat, and his own blood had begun to pound in the same fast rhythm. He very nearly lost his train of thought when her eyelids lowered and her breath began to hitch.

Still watching her, he lowered his hands to her waist and unsnapped her jeans. The sound was erotic and his fingers fumbled as he pushed down the fabric. He'd gotten them to her knees when he saw something that made his own breath hitch. Beneath those very practical jeans, she was wearing red lace panties.

He dropped to his knees, and simply stared at them. Zoë McNamara was just one surprise after another. He had no idea how long he'd knelt there before her hands covered his to push at the jeans. Minutes? Hours?

Giving his head a little shake to clear it, he said, "No. Let me." But his gaze remained fixed on the fire-engine red panties. They were a combination of lace and silk, and he was hard-pressed to remember that he was Ethan, and not Jed.

Somehow he managed to get her jeans off. But then he simply had to touch. He took his time, drawing his finger along the red lace where it rode high on her thigh. Fantasies were made of this. Jed would say that out loud. Ethan would only think it.

When he reached the apex of her thighs, he slid his fingers between them and touched the heat at her center.

"Ethan." His name came out on a sigh and her fingers dug into his shoulders.

"Spread your legs a little," he said.

She did what he asked, and sighed his name again.

This time, he drew a finger from the low waistband in the back down the crease between her cheeks until he once more reached that spot between her legs where the heat was so intense. The silk grew more wet, and he pressed against it.

Zoë began to tremble.

To steady her, he pressed the palm of his free hand against her buttocks and drew her close. "Do you want me to stop?"

Her nails dug into his shoulders. "No."

ZOË WASN'T SURE that she had spoken the word out loud. She didn't want him to stop. Ever. She put more effort into it. *"No."*

Evidently he heard her because he increased the pressure of his finger until she could feel him enter her.

Not nearly far enough. The silk of her panties was preventing him from going deep the way she wanted him to, and there was an enormous feeling of emptiness growing inside of her. It was making her tremble.

As if in response, he pressed his mouth to her waist and she felt the quick, sharp probe of his tongue in her navel. If he hadn't had her so firmly pressed against him, she was sure she would have melted into a pool on the floor.

"All night long, I've been wondering what you might be wearing under those jeans."

Zoë threaded her fingers through his hair. Her research had told her that men thought about things like that. That's why she'd bought them. Rory had convinced her that Jed would like them. For one second, she felt a little trickle of guilt. Then Ethan pushed his finger into her a little deeper.

"Ohhh," she moaned and swayed.

In one smooth movement, he rose, lifted her in his arms and carried her to the bed.

"Let's try this," he murmured as he laid her back against the pillows. He spread her legs apart and then slid down until his face was between her thighs. For a moment, he did nothing.

Zoë dug her fingers into the sheets and waited. Desire built and anticipation turned into a painful ache before he pressed his mouth to her thigh. That wasn't where she wanted him, but the string of wet, openmouthed kisses was coming closer, and closer....

For one blissful second, she felt his breath warm against the wetness of her panties. Arrows of sensation shot through her. But then he turned his attention to her other thigh.

If she could have found the strength, she would have hit him. She began to writhe on the sheets, but he clamped his hands on her thighs to hold her still. Intense pleasure mixed with the pain of wanting, needing more. "Please."

With one finger he traced her cleft and once more pressed against her center. Then he pushed his finger into her again—but still not far enough.

She arched, straining against his hands. "Please," she gasped again.

Just when she thought that she couldn't stand the delightful agony a second longer, he put his mouth where his finger had been and began to use his teeth and tongue on her. Every sensation was so intense—the heat of his breath, the press of his tongue. She could even feel the scrape of his teeth through the thin silk. Once again, flames coursed through her body, and all she could think was *more*.

MORE. HE NEEDED MORE. He had to have all of her. Jed had never before felt this driving need to take, to possess. Whatever plan he'd had to make love to her slowly had burned up in the heat that they'd created together. He retrieved a condom and got rid of his clothes. Fingers fumbling, he sheathed himself. All the while he barely took his eyes off of her. She was watching him, her eyes half-closed. Her skin was porcelain-white in the moonlight, that slash of red the only thing still covering her. She quite simply bewitched him.

Oh, yes. He wanted more. He wanted all of her. Lowering himself over her, he pushed aside the thin swatch of red silk and drove himself in.

She wrapped arms and legs around him, drawing him into her deeper and deeper. Together, they raced. When they finally reached the peak of pleasure and soared over it, he wasn't quite sure who had claimed whom.

11

JED FOUND RYDER ALONE in the kitchen of the apartment he kept above the offices of his security firm. Jensen, Ryder's office manager and sometime butler, had been waiting to give Jed the key to the elevator when he arrived.

"You look like hell," Ryder said as he shoved a mug of coffee across the counter.

Jed ran a hand through his hair and glanced down at the clothes he was wearing. He'd changed into some fresh Ethan Blair clothes that he'd had in the room, but he hadn't taken the time to shower or shave. "I wanted to get out of there before Zoë woke up."

Ryder regarded him steadily. "It saves on the awkward morning-after stuff."

"Yeah." Restless, he paced to the window as he sipped coffee. He'd hated like hell leaving her there. But what choice had he had?

The same choices he'd had when he'd dragged her into this mess, a voice at the back of his mind said.

He turned back to Ryder. "Your men are there?"

"They're waiting for her in the lobby. I sent them as

soon as you called and said you were on your way. When she comes down, they'll explain that Ethan Blair sent them."

"I want her kept safe," Jed said.

"You won't get any argument from me."

Ryder's slight emphasis on the word *me* wasn't lost on Jed.

"I know. I know that I'm the one who's put her in danger. But I'm not going to go near her again until it's over."

"You don't think she'll come looking for you?" Ryder asked.

"No." Jed took another sip of his coffee. "I told her she'd never see Ethan Blair again."

Ryder's eyes narrowed. "You didn't tell her that you and Ethan Blair are one and the same?"

"No. I was going to and then it got complicated."

Ryder shot him a look. "Sooo…what if she comes looking for Jed Calhoun?"

Jed took another drink of his coffee. "I think she's over him."

"According to Sierra, that might not be the case. She lost her concentration at work when you didn't call her."

"Sierra said that?" Jed asked.

Ryder nodded. "It got so bad, Sierra decided Zoë needed a night out—that's why they were at the Blue Pepper. She even arranged for Zoë to borrow some clothes from Sierra's sister, Rory. They're about the same size."

Had she worn that lace top hoping to see Jed again? And what about the red panties? A whirl of emotions he couldn't quite name shot through him. Or had she worn them hoping to meet someone new? "She may be over Jed Calhoun now that she's met Ethan Blair."

"Maybe you should have told her the truth."

Jed set his mug down on the counter so hard that some sloshed out. "Maybe. I told myself I was thinking about her safety. At first. Then all I was thinking about was her. I can't be in the same room with her and not lose brain cells. And I can't seem to keep my hands off of her." He paused and shot a furious look at his friend. "I don't expect you to understand. Hell, I barely understand it myself."

Ryder's grin spread across his features and turned into a laugh that filled the room. After putting down his mug, he crossed to Jed and patted him on the shoulder. "Oh, I understand all right. The same thing happened to me from the moment that I first set eyes on Sierra. I picked her up in a bar and kissed her before I even introduced myself."

Some of the anger and frustration in Jed started to ease. An odd kind of warmth moved through him as he thought of Zoë being distracted at work because of him. "So she couldn't stop thinking about me."

Ryder grinned at him. "About Jed. I wonder if she'll be thinking about Ethan now."

Jed frowned. "Just as soon as I can take a shower, wash the dye out of my hair and ditch these colored contacts, Ethan will be gone and he's not coming back."

"Too much competition, huh?"

The look in Jed's eyes had Ryder holding up both hands defensively. "I won't say another word. I promise. Just…" He backed away a few steps. "How does it feel to be in competition with yourself?"

Jed fisted his hands at his side. "It sucks." Especially when he couldn't go near her as either man.

Ryder's expression sobered. "Yes, I suppose it would."

"I have to call her as Ethan Blair and tell her that there are two men in the lobby waiting for her."

Ryder nodded. "First, why don't you show me what's in the envelope your friend Gage sent you? You did bring it?"

Jed drew the envelope out of his pocket.

Ryder spread the contents out on the counter and studied them for a moment. Then he shot a smile at Jed. "If we're lucky, we should be able to finesse our way into Bailey Montgomery's office tonight."

ZOË KNEW EVEN AS SHE drifted up through layers of sleep that she was alone in the bed. Each time that she'd drifted awake before there'd been Ethan's hard, hot body pressed against hers. And each time she'd turned to him in the night, he'd made love to her again.

Heaven help her, but she wanted him again right now. She stretched out her hand, but all she could feel was cool sheets. And the sun was shining into the room. She could feel the warmth, see it dancing beyond her eyelids. It was morning, and she didn't want to face it yet.

Fighting off her growing awareness, she concentrated hard on slipping back into the oblivion of sleep. The scent of coffee wasn't helping one bit. Opening one eye, she made out the black carafe on the nightstand and the yellow daffodil in a vase. Then the phone next to it rang.

Shoving the hair out of her eyes, Zoë sat up and grabbed the receiver. "Hello?"

"You're awake?"

Zoë drew up her knees and clasped her free arm around them. A British accent shouldn't sound so sexy, and a man's voice shouldn't be able to make her insides melt.

"Where are you?" she asked.

"I don't have much time. There are two men waiting for you in the lobby. Bodyguards. They'll be with you 24/7 until I can clear this matter up and make sure that you are safe."

Zoë didn't say anything. She wasn't sure she could get any sound past the lump in her throat.

"Take care, Zoë."

For a while she just sat there listening to the dial tone. Was every single man she spent the night with going to walk away from her?

How many more men did she intend to have a one-night stand with? Making love with two men in three days might not go into the Guinness World Records, but for her it was definitely on the wild side. And what had it gotten her?

Absolutely mind-blowing sex for one thing. And she didn't regret a moment of it.

Slowly she smiled. She'd thought that nothing could surpass what Jed Calhoun had done to her in that hammock. But last night with Ethan... Resting her head on her knees, she let the images, the feelings, wash over her. They'd made love twice more after that first time. It was the last time that played itself over in her mind. He'd been so gentle, so thorough. Just thinking about it had heat building in her again.

Shaking her head to clear it, she reached for the carafe and poured herself a cup. Instead of reliving the fantasy, she should be considering the consequences. There would be a price to pay.

Taking a sip of her coffee, Zoë made herself look around the room. Her camisole was on a nearby chair, her panties were a bright splash of red against the cream-colored carpet. The bed looked as if a battle had been fought on it.

Well, the battle was over, and now it was time to assess the damage. She'd desired and acted on those desires with two men. It wasn't as though she'd stopped wanting one of them before she'd moved on to the next one. Because she hadn't. Jed had moved on; he'd obviously stopped wanting her.

She thought of Jed Calhoun, the gray-green eyes that always seemed to be laughing, the tousled hair bleached by the sun, and those hard, demanding hands. As the thrill moved through her, an image filled her mind. Jed, wearing nothing but cutoff shorts, was leaning against a tree, willing her to come to him. If he were standing in the bedroom doorway right now, she would go to him. Better still, she would beckon him to join her in bed. Her blood was already heating and racing at the thought.

And if Ethan were standing there? In her mind, the image of Jed receded a bit, and she pictured a man with straighter posture, darker hair, and bright blue, serious eyes behind black-rimmed glasses. A hunger filled her and with it came an ache that had her gripping her knees even more tightly.

She would beckon to Ethan, too, and beg him to make love to her again—just as she'd begged him more than once during the night. Zoë shut her eyes. But she couldn't quite erase the images of the two men.

In fact, they were both walking toward the bed. She felt a lick of fire along her nerve endings. And she felt another hotter flame spring to life deep inside of her. Ethan reached her first. He knelt on the bed and taking her by the hand, drew her to her knees. She knelt facing him, her body nearly brushing against his. His eyes were so dark but she could see herself in them. Though she couldn't take her gaze away from his, she knew the moment that Jed climbed onto the bed behind her.

Ethan's hands rested at her throat, and then his mouth lowered to hers at the same moment that Jed's hands settled at her waist.

This was a fantasy, she thought. It was happening entirely in her mind. But the heat coursing through her was very real. And so were the other sensations—the gentle movement of Ethan's tongue as it danced with hers, the tremor that moved through her when Jed's hand covered her breast.

Then Jed drew her close so that she felt every hard plane and angle of his body against her back. The slap of heat nearly rocked her.

Ethan moved closer, too—until her body was pressed tightly between the two men.

She really should put a stop to this.

As if in answer to the thought, Ethan moved one hand to the nape of her neck and abruptly changed the angle of the kiss. His mouth became hard, demanding. His tongue was no longer gentle. She lifted her hands and gripped his shoulders to pull him closer. His tongue explored her mouth as if there were some flavor there that she was hiding from him and that he was bent on discovering. The sudden scrape of his teeth had her moaning.

As if determined to regain her attention, Jed slipped the hand that had been resting at her waist in between Ethan's body and hers and moved it lower and lower until he slipped his finger between her legs. Pleasure exploded through her as she began to move against the pressure he was creating.

When Ethan dragged his mouth from hers and took it on a slow journey down her throat, she said, "More."

And for the life of her, she didn't know which man she was talking to. Both of them?

Jed increased the rhythm and pressure of his finger, and Ethan moved his mouth down her throat to her breast. Pleasure built to a flashpoint. She thought she could hear murmurs, the sounds of one man and then the other saying her name. The world narrowed to the two men and the sensations they brought to her.

They could have asked anything of her and she would have given it. She wanted—no, she needed—both of them inside of her. Right now.

"Don't stop. Please."

It was Ethan's hair she shoved her hands into. It was Jed's teeth that sank into that spot he'd discovered at the base of her neck. It was Ethan's hands that slid around and began to knead her buttocks. But it was Jed's fingers that slid into her and began to move.

Zoë began to move, too, and the orgasm built slowly in a tidal wave that widened as it gathered force. Pleasure burst through her in a series of explosions that sent her flying and had her crying out one man's name and then the other. And then she was falling back onto the bed.

Trapped in the aftershocks of the orgasm, she couldn't stop trembling and she had to concentrate on breathing in and out. For a while there, oxygen hadn't seemed important at all. Nothing else had but the two men.

Two men. What had happened to her? She'd never expected her decision to make love just once to Jed Calhoun would lead to this.

Now her life seemed to consist of bed hopping from one fantasy to another—making love with a perfect stranger, making love with two men at once.

What was next?

Opening her eyes, she aimed a look in the direction of the heavens. "That was strictly rhetorical. Forget I asked."

Then she risked a cautious look around the bedroom. Yes, she was alone. Her little romp with Jed and Ethan had been a pure fantasy. Sitting up, she pounded a fist into the bed because she should be feeling relieved about that, not disappointed.

But she was going to get a grip. She probably wouldn't see Ethan ever again. But she would have to try to see Jed again. The realization had her opening her eyes wide. Until this minute, she'd completely forgotten the envelope that Rad had delivered with the wine bottle last night. Quickly, she crawled out of the bed and located her bag in the living room of the suite. But she didn't find the envelope.

It had been there when she'd arrived. She'd checked while Ethan had been in the bathroom. Immediately she began to search the suite. In the bedroom, she dropped down on her hands and knees and looked under the bed, the chair and the nightstand. Then she rose and conducted a thorough search of the bathroom and finally the living room.

Ten minutes later she had convinced herself that the envelope hadn't fallen on the floor or slipped beneath the cushions on the sofas. It wasn't anywhere in the suite.

The message that someone had given her to deliver to Jed was definitely gone. With a sinking heart, Zoë sat down on the edge of the coffee table and stared out the window. There was only one person who could have taken the envelope. Ethan Blair.

Clearly, she was still wearing rose-colored glasses when it came to men. Ethan Blair must have known she had that envelope all the time. She'd been on the patio when Rad had delivered it, and there were spaces between the screens. She would have been visible from the street.

She thought of his words: *I felt the same thing…. Will you let me make love to you?*

Had he seduced her to get the envelope intended for Jed Calhoun? Did the two men have some connection that she wasn't aware of?

There was only one thing she was sure of. She had to warn Jed.

And two of Ethan's men were sitting in the lobby waiting for her to come down so that they could act as her bodyguards.

That wasn't going to happen. Not until she figured out what was going on. Straightening her shoulders, Zoë gathered her clothes and began to dress.

BAILEY MONTGOMERY liked things to make sense. Tapping her foot, she stared out the window of her office and once again went over the information she was certain of.

Gage Sinclair had arranged to meet Jed Calhoun at the Blue Pepper. That much she'd gotten from the tap she'd put on his phone. What she didn't know were the details of what Jed had asked Gage to bring with him in that envelope.

But Gage hadn't made contact with Jed. She was sure of that. The only person Gage had spoken to was the bartender. George was his name, and he'd been very close-mouthed when she'd questioned him about Zoë that night. The only thing he'd let slip was that she was Dr. Sierra Gibbs's research assistant at Georgetown. But that had been enough for her to track down Zoë's address.

Perhaps Jed hadn't shown up. She certainly hadn't spotted him.

But then Jed Calhoun was reputed to be a master of disguise. He could easily have been there and she'd missed him. She'd expected to finger Jed by watching Gage Sinclair. So either Gage had spotted her and aborted the meet, or Jed Calhoun had never intended to show up.

Either way, Zoë McNamara was the key to her finding Jed Calhoun. Gage had sent the envelope to her. Why her?

That was the question that had Bailey stumped. Once she'd gotten to the office, she'd accessed Zoë's personnel file and verified her memory that Zoë had worked almost exclusively for Hadley Richards during the two months that she'd been at the CIA. There was nothing in her file that indicated she'd been anything but an excellent analyst.

But there'd been those rumors she was having an affair with Hadley Richards just before she'd resigned. One thing was certain: she had to find Zoë and talk to her.

But the woman hadn't come home last night. Bailey

glanced at her watch. It was nearly noon, and she hadn't shown up at her house or the university.

Number one on her agenda when she'd left Zoë McNamara's apartment had been to hire a P.I. she knew and trusted to stake out Zoë McNamara's house and office.

Bailey couldn't recall ever talking to Zoë while she'd worked for Hadley, but she'd seen her every now and then. She'd been mousier-looking back then, and she certainly hadn't seemed to be Hadley's usual type. Bailey's heart went out to her. A young woman like Zoë wouldn't have had a clue as to what she was dealing with when it came to a shark like Hadley Richards.

Now she was in a Ph.D. program at Georgetown and working as Dr. Sierra Gibbs's research assistant. From what Bailey had been able to gather, the two women were doing some kind of sex research.

The only other thing she could think of to check was the work that Zoë had been doing for Hadley Richards during those two months. Her assistant, Margaret, was getting that information for her right now.

When Bailey realized that her tapping foot had picked up its rhythm, she stilled it, and her gaze shifted to her image in the window.

A night of tossing and turning and trying to make sense of stuff that didn't easily separate into neat categories didn't contribute to the General Patton image she liked to project while she was in the office. The gray linen suit and the bright turquoise blouse didn't quite negate the dark circles underneath her eyes.

And the frosting on the cake was the fact that she felt as if she was being followed. Oh, she hadn't spotted anyone, but the prickling sensation now and then at the back of her neck was a sure sign. She'd sensed it when she'd left Zoë McNamara's apartment last night and then again this morning when she'd come to work.

The hell of it was, she hadn't been able to spot anyone. Whoever was tailing her was good.

Swallowing a sigh, she turned back to her desk just as Hadley Richards knocked once and strode into her office. She raised her brows. "I didn't know you had an appointment."

"I do now," he said as he closed the door and then strolled forward to settle himself in a chair.

She remained standing.

"I want to continue the discussion about that job you were supposed to do in Colombia."

Her brows shot up. "You mean the job I *did* in Colombia? I don't know what more I can do to reassure you that—"

"What were you doing at the Blue Pepper in Georgetown last night?" Hadley asked.

Her mind was racing as Bailey sat down at her desk and met his gaze steadily. "I was having drinks with friends."

Hadley leaned back in his chair. "Gage Sinclair was there, too. He's one of two men that Jed Calhoun might have contacted—if he wasn't dead."

Bailey said nothing. But once again she was reminded that Hadley Richards was not a man she could afford to underestimate.

"Do you know what I suspect?" Hadley asked.

"No."

"I believe that you're not as certain as you want me to believe that our dead man hasn't risen. And you're watching Gage to see if he's been contacted. Has he been?"

"No. How many times do I have to tell you that the last time I saw Calhoun he was lying dead in an alley in Bogotá?"

Hadley leaned forward. "Until I believe it. If you're wrong, or if you're lying, I expect you to find him and correct the mistake."

Bailey said nothing, but the "or else" hung in the air between them.

Hadley rose and moved to the door, turning back only when he reached it. "I'll be watching you."

Well, shit, Bailey thought as the door closed behind Had. He was already watching her. She hadn't been followed to the Blue Pepper. She was certain of that, but Hadley must have had someone tailing Gage Sinclair. And he must have had her followed when she left the restaurant. That would explain the strange feeling she'd had that she was being watched.

Bailey frowned. It also meant that someone had followed her to Zoë McNamara's apartment. That meant she had to find the connection between Zoë and Jed Calhoun before Hadley Richards did.

Bailey rose and paced back to the window. Clearly,

Hadley Richards didn't trust her. If he became convinced that she'd bungled the hit on Jed Calhoun six months ago, it wasn't likely that he was going to rely on her to take care of it this time, despite his instructions for her to correct her mistake. The question was how much time did she have?

She glanced around her office. She certainly wasn't going to make any arrangements from here.

After opening her desk, she pressed a button and when the false bottom of the drawer snapped up, she retrieved two files that contained everything she knew about Jed Calhoun and Frank Medici. After placing them in her bag, she added the new file on Zoë McNamara. Then Bailey moved into her outer office. Number one on her agenda was to find out who was following her and lose them.

"Margaret," she said to the neat, prim woman behind the reception desk. "I have some appointments that will keep me out of the office for the rest of the day. Did you get that information I asked for?"

"Right here."

When Margaret handed her the file that contained the work that Zoë had done for Hadley Richards, Bailey glanced at the first page and saw it instantly. This was the link she was looking for—and it didn't bode well for Jed Calhoun.

12

Zoë PEERED OUT the back window of the taxi for the fifth time since she'd left the Woodbridge Hotel. As far as she could tell, she wasn't being followed. She'd avoided Ethan's men, who were waiting for her in the lobby, by taking the stairs, exiting the hotel through a side door and walking five blocks to hail a taxi.

If she didn't trust Ethan, she could hardly trust any men he'd sent to watch over her. And she wasn't about to lead them to Jed. If she could find him.

She turned around and leaned back against the seat, trying to relax. Her work at the CIA hadn't involved any cloak-and-dagger stuff. What sleuthing she'd done had been from the safety of her desk. Of course, there'd been that little hum in the blood when she'd broken into something that was supposed to be "protected." But there'd been nothing to compare to the adrenaline rush she'd experienced last night, escaping from real live thugs.

Or being seduced by a sexy James Bond type.

Every time she thought of Ethan, the tension in her

stomach knotted tighter. And dammit, her heartbeat quickened. Why? The man had made love to her to get the envelope that had been addressed to Jed. That was pretty obvious. He'd used her, and she'd fallen for it. She wasn't sure what made her angrier—that she'd been so gullible or that if she ran into Ethan right now, he might have very little trouble seducing her again.

Zoë shut her eyes and sighed. What in the world was happening to her? Three weeks ago, she'd had a nice, orderly life. Her goals had been clear, and she'd been proceeding in a straightforward path to achieving them.

She'd also been bored to death. And her sex life had consisted of doing research and engaging in daydreams with a fantasy lover—code name Lucifer!

Then she'd met Jed Calhoun, and everything had changed. She'd never experienced that kind of instant and powerful attraction to a man before. Making love with Jed had triggered some sexual freedom in her that she couldn't seem to get under control. She'd taken a bite of the forbidden apple. And then a second.

Worse than that, she couldn't seem to summon up even a shred of regret that she'd given in to temptation. In less than three days, two handsome, exciting and very different men had desired her and made love to her as if they'd meant it. She hugged the knowledge close and found she couldn't prevent the delight that coursed through her.

She'd spent most of her life trying to be her parents—intellectual, reserved, detached. Their entire existence was focused on getting published, getting grants, getting appointed to prestigious positions. She was pretty sure she didn't want to go back to that kind of life.

And she certainly didn't want to go back to her fantasy lover. Zoë frowned. Although both Jed Calhoun and Ethan Blair shared many qualities with Lucifer.

As the taxi swerved into one of the traffic circles D.C. was famous for, she tried to push all three men firmly out of her mind. Right now, she had to concentrate on letting Ryder Kane know that someone had stolen whatever was in that envelope intended for Jed Calhoun. It was the least she could do.

A glance at the nearest street sign told her that Ryder Kane's office was only a few blocks away. While she'd dressed and made her escape from the hotel, she'd decided that if anyone knew how to contact Jed, Ryder would. As the taxi pulled to the curb, she glanced up at the building that housed not only Ryder's D.C. office but also his living space on the top floor. It was in that apartment that she'd first met Jed. Pushing the memory away, she paid the driver and stepped out onto the sidewalk.

She would give Ryder the information and let him pass it on to Jed. That would be the end of it.

Then she would go back to her office and make some decisions about her life.

GAGE SINCLAIR glanced at his watch for the fourth time in as many minutes. He'd been tailing Bailey Montgomery for two hours, ever since she'd left her office at Langley at 10:00 a.m. His hadn't been the only car following hers. She'd eliminated the other tail in less than ten minutes, and then she'd executed a few maneuvers with her car that told him she suspected she was still being followed.

But she hadn't shaken him. He knew a few maneuvers himself.

When Bailey had eventually headed toward Georgetown, he'd expected her to stop at either Zoë McNamara's apartment or her office. That's when Agent Montgomery surprised him. Instead of checking either place, she'd parked her car on a commercial street that boasted a cluster of trendy boutiques and she'd gone shopping.

Thoroughly intrigued, he'd slipped into a parking space three cars down from hers, turned off his engine, rolled down his windows and waited. What was she up to? The Bailey Montgomery that he knew—and he'd known her for eight years now—wasn't the kind of woman to take time off to go shopping on a workday.

The first store she'd entered had been an antique gallery. Gage shifted his position and glanced at his watch. She'd been in there for fifteen minutes now. If she'd come here to meet with someone, they were either late or she was early. And just who was she meeting with? He knew from his own men that Zoë McNamara hadn't returned to either her apartment or her office on the Georgetown campus. He also knew that Bailey was undoubtedly keeping just as close an eye on Zoë.

Gage agreed with Jed that Bailey Montgomery held the key to the reason that he was being framed for Frank Medici's murder. But Gage didn't think that Bailey had played a part in the frame. He'd done his research on her before he'd actively recruited her. She was smart, capable and a straight shooter. She would follow orders like a good soldier, but she wouldn't follow them blindly. That characteristic had played a huge part in his decision to recruit her.

That and the fact that she had a clever and creative mind. He had no doubt she'd planted the bug he'd discovered in his office phone. His lips curved in a smile at the thought. How in the hell had she managed it? He had some pretty effective security arrangements in place. He intended to ask her—eventually. Right now, he had to focus on why she'd bugged his office in the first place. It had to mean that she'd suspected Jed Calhoun would get in touch with him. And that meant that she'd known Jed was alive.

The question that intrigued him most was *when* she'd learned that little fact. Or had she known it all along? Had she purposely left Jed Calhoun alive in that alley?

As Bailey exited the antique store and moved toward her car, he considered getting out, walking up to her and asking her that very question.

But he knew from the dossier he'd compiled on her eight years ago that she wasn't a woman who trusted easily. So he decided to wait. There was always the chance that Jed's plan of breaking into her office and looking for files would work.

In the meantime, he enjoyed watching her stride down the sidewalk. She moved with a quick, athletic grace that wasted neither time nor energy. He admired both that and the way she dressed more like a fashion plate than a CIA agent. The tailored pants and jacket were a pale gray pinstripe that did nothing to suggest masculinity, and the bright blue blouse she wore beneath it hinted at everything feminine. She wore her blond hair at chin length in one of those smooth, sleek haircuts that a man fantasized about messing up.

She still had the same self-confidence and style that she'd had when they'd first met. It had attracted him then, and it attracted him now.

The realization that he still had a strong yen for Bailey Montgomery had struck him full force last night at the Blue Pepper. He'd figured the time that had passed and the fact that he hadn't seen her in so long would have taken care of it. But from the moment he'd spotted her in the bar, the attraction had been powerful and electric, just like before. Sooner or later, he was going to have to give that some thought.

Right now, he'd better concentrate on the job. Grabbing his paper off the seat, he drew it up to block her view of his face as she turned from depositing a package in her car and strode down the sidewalk in his direction. Directly across from where he was parked, she took a quick right turn into another store. A swift glance told him it sold women's undergarments—the kind designed to destroy a man's brain cells.

His gaze lingered on the frothy bits of lace and silk on display in the window. Though he'd never given much thought to what Bailey Montgomery wore beneath those neatly tailored suits, he did now.

Through the window, he watched her select a handful of creamy-colored lace and walk to the back of the store. To a dressing room, he supposed. That was all the stimulation his imagination needed to slip into a fantasy. He might have put some effort into stifling it, but what the hell. Tailing people had some very dull moments. A man had to keep his mind occupied somehow.

Leaning back against the seat, Gage cleared his mind and pictured Bailey Montgomery slipping out of her jacket and draping it over the back of a chair. Next came the belt. He pictured her unbuckling it and drawing it slowly out of the loops. Her hands, with those long, slender fingers, would deal with the buttons and then the zipper. A pleasant warmth stole through him as he imagined her lowering the zipper, inch by inch. The slacks slid into a pool around her feet.

One look at those long, slender legs made Gage's mouth water, and heat flooded his body. When her fingers began to unfasten her blouse, his blood began to hammer in a rhythm that picked up speed as each button slipped free.

Finally, the blue silk joined the slacks at her feet. Now all she wore was a wispy black lace bra and panties.

His mouth went dry as he absorbed the contrast of black lace and skin the color of alabaster. It would feel smooth as glass, soft as rose petals. A man would give up a lot to get his hands on it. To explore it slowly and mold every inch of it.

He could even smell her now. It was the same elusive scent she'd had all those years ago—something exotic and unexpected, like a flower one might come upon in a steamy, hot jungle.

"Put your hands on the wheel and keep them there."

The clipped, no-nonsense tone snapped him back from his erotic fantasy, and he swiveled his head to stare at a fully clothed Bailey Montgomery. She had a small revolver pointed at him.

"I'll use it. Put your hands on the steering wheel, Sinclair," Bailey repeated as she used her free hand to release the lock and open the passenger door.

That was the trouble with fantasies, Gage thought. There was always a price to pay. If he hadn't been so distracted by her he would have known just what she was doing. And he had to hand it to her, it was a very skillful maneuver. She'd led him here so she could get his license plate and get a trace run on it. Then she'd made her move.

He sent her a slow, admiring and, he hoped, charming smile. "You're not going to pull that trigger on the man who recruited you and trained you."

Her brows shot up. "Want to bet? And don't forget, you're the one who drilled me on how to cover up a hit and make it look like an accident."

Gage sighed. "Something or other in my past is always coming back to bite me in the butt."

"I want to know why you're following me."

"I want to know what you were doing at the Blue Pepper last night. Why don't you get in and we'll trade information?"

With a quick nod, she settled herself in the seat beside him, then said, "You first. Why are you following me?"

"Since I have to keep my hands on the wheel, how about I drive to a place I know and I buy you lunch while we talk."

"And why would I want to do that?" she asked.

"Because it's damned hot in this car, and I'm hungry. Plus, I'm likely to be more cooperative with a full stomach."

She regarded him steadily.

"C'mon, Agent Montgomery. For old times' sake. What do you say?"

Bailey hesitated for only one more moment. "I choose the place and you pick up the tab."

He shot her a grin as he pulled the car onto the street. "It's a date."

JED CALHOUN WIPED the steam off the bathroom mirror and studied his reflection until he was sure that every trace of Ethan Blair was gone. He ran his fingers through his hair three times until he was satisfied that the style was back to normal, albeit shorter. The only other part of Ethan that remained was the bandage on his upper arm.

He'd replaced the one that Zoë had put on him, and the job he'd done wasn't half as neat as hers had been.

Zoë. He couldn't seem to get her out of his mind. He pulled on a T-shirt and briefs that he'd copped from Ryder's dresser. But he'd have to wear "Ethan's" slacks. The idea of that brought a quick frown to his face.

If he could have avoided wearing anything of Ethan's, he would have, but Ryder's jeans wouldn't fit him. His friend was a bit shorter and wider at the waist. In the shower, it had struck him that his efforts to get rid of all traces of Ethan Blair were all because of Zoë.

He couldn't help thinking of Ethan as a rival. He was jealous of a man he'd created, a man who didn't exist, a man who was him. If he could have had his wish, he'd go find Zoë right now and make love to her over and over until she completely forgot that Ethan Blair ever existed.

He met his eyes in the mirror and slowly shook his head again. Insane. That's what he was. Somehow the woman had gotten into his system and attacked his brain cells. He should avoid her like the plague. And he would—at least until he solved his more pressing problems. Plan A was getting into Bailey Montgomery's office tonight. If that failed…he was going to have a little heart-to-heart with Bailey herself.

On that note, he opened the bathroom door and stepped into the hall. At the same moment, the doors of Ryder's private elevator door slid open, and Zoë walked through them.

Jed stopped dead in his tracks. His first thought was that he'd conjured her up. His gaze was drawn to her lacey camisole. She was wearing the same clothes she'd been wearing the night before. The memory had his blood heating. And the red lace panties? Was she wearing those, also? For some ridiculous reason it bothered him that Ethan Blair had seen them first.

"I…" she said, finally breaking the silence that stretched between them. She turned as if to run, but the elevator doors had already slid shut. Whirling back, she scurried for the kitchen area and put the small island between them. Then she faced him and met his eyes. "Ryder didn't tell me you were here. He just said to come up and make myself at home." She raised her hands and dropped them. "I don't expect you're happy to see me."

She wasn't a figment of his imagination. This was the real Zoë, nervous as a mouse. Cute as a button. He wanted to eat her right up. And for some reason her nerves eased his own tension as he moved forward. "Why would you think that I wouldn't want to see you?"

"Because…" She paused to twist her hands together. "You didn't call."

The phone rang.

"Speaking of calls, hold that thought." Jed circled the counter, and keeping his eyes on Zoë, picked up the phone on the wall behind the island. "Yeah?"

"Zoë's on her way up," Ryder said.

"She's here. Thanks for the warning."

"I tried, but you didn't answer."

"I was in the shower."

"Well, she gave my men at the hotel the slip. I didn't think you'd want her wandering around D.C. without some kind of protection. Besides, she has something to tell you. And don't you have something you want to tell her?"

Jed could hear the suppressed laughter in Ryder's voice.

"This is your chance to dig yourself out of that hole you're in," Ryder continued. "Or one of them at least."

"Thanks." Jed hung up the phone. There would be a time when he'd get even with his friend, but not now. There might also be a time when he'd confess to Zoë that he was Ethan Blair. But not until he'd taken the opportunity to wipe that man right out of her mind.

He took a step toward her, and Zoë stiffened. But she didn't scurry to the other side of the counter this time.

"I think…you should get dressed," she said.

Jed glanced down at his briefs and remembered that he'd been on his way to get his slacks out of the guest room. But he wasn't about to put on Ethan's clothes. She might recognize them. "First I want to finish the conversation we were having just before Ryder called."

She frowned. "We weren't having a conversation."

"Sure we were. It was fascinating." He moved toward her and she backed into the island.

"You didn't think I would be happy to see you. Why is that?" he asked.

"Because you didn't call," she repeated.

"Call?"

"Forget it." She waved a hand. "We agreed that making love was a one-time thing. You had no obligation to call. I understand that."

He moved another step closer so that their bodies were nearly brushing. "But you wanted me to call? You wanted to see me again?"

"I—yes."

Triumph moved through him. "I've missed you."

Her eyes widened, and the little pulse at the base of her throat began to beat. "You have?"

He traced one finger along the lace at the top of her camisole. "I've been fantasizing again."

Zoë swallowed hard. "Really?"

"Mmm, hmm." The image in his mind right now was of taking her on that island that she had backed herself against. While he continued to trace the lace of her camisole, he used his free hand to nudge her toward him so that he only had to lower his head to whisper in her ear, "Want to know what I have in mind?"

"No." She placed a hand on his chest.

He drew back then. "No?"

"I can't. I came here to tell you something…. You're making me forget it."

"Can't we talk about it later?" he asked as he brushed kisses along her jawline.

She increased the pressure of her hand on his chest until he drew back again.

"You might not want to make love to me once I tell

you. Last night when I was at the Blue Pepper someone gave me an envelope addressed to you. And then I left with this other man. He…I…" She paused and began to bite on her bottom lip. "We ended up spending the night together."

"You spent the night with another man?"

Heat flooded her cheeks. "Yes. And he took the envelope. It must have been what he was after all along. He must have seen Rad deliver it to me. That must be why he approached me and…I'm so sorry. The envelope must have been important. And I—you…that's what I wanted Ryder to tell you. I thought you should know. I'll go now."

Would she ever stop surprising him? He hadn't expected a confession. And she felt she'd betrayed him by letting Ethan steal the envelope? The pleasure that gave him added fuel to the fire that had burst to life the moment he'd seen her. He took the hand she had pressed against his chest and raised it to his lips.

She simply stared at him.

"Answer one thing for me?"

She nodded. "Okay."

"Let me make love to you again?"

13

ZOË FELT HER THOUGHTS slipping away as quickly as if the plug holding them in her head had been pulled. There wasn't room for thoughts, not when there were so many feelings pouring through her. Delight. Surprise. And desire. There would always be desire with this man. But she really shouldn't be giving in to it. If he wasn't standing so close, if her head wasn't filled with images of making love with him, if her heart wasn't beating so hard, she might be able to say no.

"I…we…"

"Okay, let me put it another way," Jed said. "You're used to analyzing data, right?"

She nodded.

"Facts, evidence, that kind of stuff?"

"Yes." How was she supposed to think clearly when his mouth hovered a breath away from hers?

"Try this. I want you." He pressed his lips against the corner of her mouth. "You want me." He moved his mouth to the other corner. "Don't you?"

"Mmmm." The feelings he was stirring in her were

glorious. She wanted to drown in them. But she really shouldn't.

"Come with me, Zoë."

Oh, she wanted to. More than anything, she wanted this man—his touch, his mouth, his body pressed against hers. Hadn't she come here secretly hoping that Jed would be here with Ryder?

Drawing back, she met his eyes and saw some, if not all, of what she was feeling. Taking a deep breath, she said, "Yes."

She saw triumph flash into his eyes. Then he lowered his mouth to hers before either one of them had a chance to think about it anymore. Zoë let the feelings swamp her. She'd never tasted hunger like this before. She wasn't sure if it was his or her own or a combination. And beneath it she tasted a desperation that was also new. This was not the playful man who'd made love with her in the hammock. His mouth was more demanding. His teeth nipped and scraped, sending chills and fire along her nerve endings. And his hands—they were impatient, rough, thrilling. He could have anything he asked. The realization frightened her, thrilled her. All she wanted to do was give and give.

She was vaguely aware of him pulling her camisole over her head. She pulled at the snap of her jeans, but he stilled her hands.

"Let me," he said as he opened the zipper and pushed her jeans down her hips. Then, for a moment, his hands paused, and his voice was hoarse. "You're not wearing any panties again."

"No." The word was barely audible. She drew in a huge gulp of air. "I didn't have a chance…to stop by my apartment…for fresh clothes."

He tipped her chin up so that she met his eyes. "Zoë McNamara, you're my perfect fantasy girl."

"Really?"

"This is twice now that you haven't worn panties. I'll never be able to be in the same room with you and not wonder."

"You've got a dirty mind."

He grinned at her as he slipped his hand between her thighs and found her heat. "Guilty as charged. But surely you can see the advantage? The ease of access?"

"Mmm." She more than saw it. She was experiencing exactly what he was talking about. His finger was moving slowly, sliding deeper and then withdrawing just before it got close enough. Zoë couldn't even remember to breathe. On some level, she was aware that he'd gotten rid of her jeans. But his finger continued to move. And so did his mouth. He nibbled a slow string of kisses along her jawline until he reached her ear.

"How do you feel about making love on a kitchen counter?" he asked just before he drew her earlobe between his teeth.

"Mmm." She couldn't even seem to form a word, not with the waves of heat shooting through her. Not with those clever fingers bringing her closer and closer. Then suddenly his hand wasn't moving.

"Don't stop."

HE WASN'T GOING TO STOP. He didn't think he could. But he wanted more. "Open your eyes, Zoë."

She did. And he watched a shock of pleasure fill her eyes as he slipped two fingers into her. Her warm, moist response dampened his hand, and he felt those hot, slick muscles close around his fingers, tempting him with a taste of what it was going to feel like when he finally entered her.

"Don't stop," she said again, arching against him.

He held his hand still. "Say my name."

Her eyes were half-closed, but her gaze was steady on his. "Jed."

That one sound pulled at what was left of his control. He wanted her *now*. It was taking all of his strength not to drag her to the floor. And it wasn't just some crazy jealousy of his alter ego that was triggering the intense rush of hunger and need he was feeling. It was the woman.

Withdrawing his fingers, he lifted her and settled her on the edge of the island countertop. "Wrap your legs around me, Zoë."

She did, but when he started to push down his briefs, she stilled his hands.

"Let me," she said, echoing his words, and she took the length of him into her hand.

He sucked in a sharp breath as pleasure knifed

through him. He glanced down at those narrow hands, the long fingers wrapped around him, and he nearly came. "Put me inside of you."

She guided him right to her entrance. He felt the hot velvet enclose just the tip of his penis. His hands gripped her hips, and he was about to draw her closer when his brain cleared enough to remember. "Protection." But he wasn't sure he could pull away, wasn't sure he could walk to the duffel bag that held the condoms.

"My bag."

Jed reached for it, found the package and somehow managed to sheathe himself.

Zoë locked her legs more tightly around him and shifted closer to the edge of the counter. "Take me now, Jed."

He obliged her by thrusting into her in one hard stroke. "You're my dream come true, Zoë."

He kissed her then, and she began to convulse around him, pulling him in even deeper. Digging his fingers into her hips, he began to drive into her harder, faster, riding a wave of pleasure that took him higher and higher, growing in intensity until it overpowered him and sent him crashing into a world of ecstasy.

BAILEY USED one of the napkins she'd grabbed at the hot dog stand and wiped off the seat of the park bench before she sat down. The Washington Mall was crowded with summer tourists, families mostly. A couple strolled by with a double baby stroller. One of the occupants was crying. Behind them a little girl was whining to be carried. Once her daddy scooped her up, she was all smiles. Most of the pedestrians were headed up the path to join the long lines at the Washington Monument.

Gage handed her one of the loaded hot dogs he was carrying and then passed her the root beer she'd ordered. "You're a surprising woman, Bailey Montgomery."

"Because I lured you into Georgetown and threatened you with a gun?" She bit into her hot dog and enjoyed the explosion of flavors on her tongue—almost as much as she'd enjoyed getting the drop on Gage Sinclair.

Much less enjoyable was her realization that the man still had an effect on her senses. The years hadn't changed that. Nor had the years seemed to change him. But she'd had plenty of time to outgrow a "crush." What she felt now, she wasn't sure.

"Well, there's that. But I should have seen it coming. More than most people, I'm acquainted with your background and your abilities. What I was thinking was that you're a cheap date."

Bailey shot him a look. "This isn't a date."

He waved that aside with his free hand. "Whatever. The point is I offered to pay, and I was expecting you to insist on lunch at the Four Seasons complete with French champagne. And I'm also surprised that you like your hot dogs fully loaded."

She took another bite and spoke around the mouthful. "It's the only way."

"No argument there." Gage took a healthy bite of his

own hot dog. "But why here? Why not take my credit card for a ride at someplace trendy and expensive?"

She shot him a serious look. "Someone might see us at a place like the Four Seasons, and I don't think it's a good idea for us to be seen together right now."

Gage bit into his hot dog and chewed thoughtfully. Then he took a swallow of his coffee. "Your boss, Hadley Richards, eats lunch at the Four Seasons at least three times a week. He also spends the occasional night there when he doesn't want to drive back to his home in Virginia. You don't want him to see us together."

Bailey studied him. She hadn't quite decided if she could trust Gage Sinclair or not. But she badly wanted to. "You keep tabs on Had?"

Gage licked mustard off his thumb. "I like to keep tabs on people I don't trust." He turned to face her then. "You don't completely trust me right now. And the feeling is mutual. Why don't you tell me why you have doubts about me, and I'll return the favor?"

Bailey took another bite of her hot dog while she considered. Finally she decided that there was no reason not to follow his suggestion. "Why were you following me?"

"Uh-uh. Explanations first and then questions." He sipped his coffee and waited.

Bailey studied him for a moment. She'd forgotten how dark and blue his eyes were. They'd always reminded her of sapphires. She had trusted the man who'd recruited her and trained her. But she hadn't seen him face-to-face since he'd left the CIA seven years ago.

He'd come close to death and sometimes that changed a man. But she was already walking on eggshells, and she had a feeling that time was running out on her.

"Go with your gut instinct, Montgomery."

That was exactly what he'd said to her on the first case they'd worked on together. Besides, what choice did she have? Taking a deep breath, she said, "I know that you went to the Blue Pepper last night to meet Jed Calhoun."

"You tapped my phone," Gage said. "I located the bug this morning."

"I'm not the only one who knew you were there to meet him."

That had him studying her. "You were followed?"

"I doubt it. Perhaps there were two taps on your phone."

Gage shook his head. "No. There was only one. I did a thorough search. Someone must have followed you."

She shook her head. "I've been thinking about that, and I don't think so. I was careful. I was thinking that someone might have followed you."

"Not a chance," Gage said.

Bailey wiped her fingers with a napkin. "Well, we were spotted there. My boss told me that much this morning. He either knows or strongly suspects that Jed Calhoun is alive and here in D.C. And he's keeping an eye on me."

"It didn't take you long to shake them loose when you left your office this morning." Gage licked mustard off his thumb and began to gather up the trash. "Let's take a walk."

When she rose, he took her arm, steering her across the grass and away from the steady stream of pedestrian traffic on the pathway.

"So why is Hadley Richards having you followed? Word has it that you're his golden girl."

Bailey snorted. "Hardly. It's my suspicion that I'm right in line to be his scapegoat." She stopped then and waited for him to face her. "I want you to tell me that you're not working for him."

He met her eyes steadily. "I'll tell you the same thing I told you seven years ago when we finished your training. People can lie. In the end the only thing you can trust is your instincts."

"You also said that if I couldn't trust anyone, couldn't let myself go with anyone, I'd never last long in this business."

"That, too."

She'd been relying on her instincts ever since Hadley Richards had walked into her office and assigned her the task of taking out Jed Calhoun. And her instinct now was to trust Gage Sinclair. Jed Calhoun trusted him. She could only pray they wouldn't both be betrayed.

Turning, she began to walk again. "Since Hadley knows or suspects Jed is alive, he also knows now that I didn't take him out six months ago in Bogotá."

This time it was Gage's turn to stop and turn her to face him. "What went wrong?"

She lifted her chin. "Nothing. I made sure the hit didn't happen. Of course, I had to make it look good.

Hadley handpicked the marksman he sent with me, but I told him I would get Jed into that alley, and he was only to shoot him in the shoulder. I said I wanted to take him out. I shot Jed in the leg, and then I arranged for Jed to be taken to a private hospital. I made sure that he had papers to get out of the country once he recovered."

"Even under orders, you didn't carry out the hit?"

"No."

"Why did you do that?"

"Because I don't believe that Jed Calhoun killed Frank Medici. I believe he was framed."

Gage sent her a slow smile. "Well, we're on the same page there."

She began to walk again. "The problem is I don't know by whom or why. The evidence against Jed is very strong. I need to see him. I'm afraid that Hadley won't stop until Jed is dead. I've got some files with me that he should see. Maybe he can find something that I'm not seeing."

Gage laughed then, and the rich sound carried on the air.

"What?" Bailey asked.

"What if I told you that Jed is planning on breaking into your office tonight to look for Frank Medici's file and the one you must have on him?"

She blinked. "How does he expect to break into CIA headquarters?"

Gage grinned at her. "I still do consulting work there, so I gave him the blueprints along with some ID badges and a few codes. If there are any other blocks, I'm sure that his friend Ryder Kane will get through them."

"It'll be a waste of their time. I've got the files right here in my bag."

"I think I'm in love with you," Gage said, taking her arm and turning her back to where he parked his car.

"Where are we going?" Bailey asked.

"How about a wedding chapel in Las Vegas? Or are you the type of woman who prefers a big wedding?"

She shot him a narrow-eyed look. "Seriously, where are we going?"

Gage sighed. "Well, if we can't go to Vegas…what if I told you that I might know where Jed Calhoun is right now?"

She sent him a smile, the first one she'd given him. "Then I'd say lead the way."

JED SLID A BELT through a pair of jeans he'd pulled out of Ryder's closet and gave himself a long look in the mirror. At least now the pants wouldn't fall down. He was going to tell Zoë he was Ethan Blair, but he wanted to set the confession up first so that she'd understand.

But would she? That was the question that set off flutters of panic in his stomach. He began to pace back and forth in the space at the foot of Ryder's bed. She might be hurt. Of course, she would be. The woman had very little confidence in herself sexually. She'd probably think he'd used her just for laughs. Hell, maybe she had a right to that opinion. It had started out that way. He'd wanted her out of his system. And if plan A had worked out, that would have been the end of it.

But what was between them hadn't ended. And now things had changed. He stopped to look at his image again. *He* had changed. And how in the hell was he supposed to tell her all that when he was still a "dead" man?

The phone rang. After striding to the bedside table, Jed picked up the receiver. "Yeah?"

"Is the coast clear or do you need more time?" Ryder asked, amusement clear in his voice.

"Give me another hour," Jed said. A little pressure might be just what he needed to spill the truth to Zoë. "By the way, I've borrowed some of your clothes."

"Not ready to appear yet in your Ethan duds?"

Jed frowned. "I'm going to tell her. Actually, I'm going to tell her everything. Thanks to me, she's involved in this right up to her pretty little neck. She deserves to know why I almost got her killed last night."

"You won't get an argument from me on that score."

"I just have to figure out a way to do it. I don't want to hurt her."

Ryder's laugh was soft. "'Oh, what a tangled web we weave, When first we practice to deceive!'"

"Thanks for the support," Jed muttered.

"Oh, you've got that all right. You're sloppy in love with her, pal. Those of us who've already taken the fall love company."

Jed dropped the phone as if it had turned red-hot in his hand. *In love?* No way. He wanted Zoë more than he'd wanted any other woman. He cared for her. He wanted to protect her. Panic fluttered again in his stomach. She might be driving him crazy. But that didn't mean he was in love with her.

Besides, when he told her that last night he'd seduced her as Ethan Blair, she would likely never speak to him again. He ran a hand through his hair. No, that wasn't going to happen. He knew how to handle a woman.

Turning, he strode toward the door. He was going to cook her a good meal, tell her all about the mess he was in, and then—when she was feeling sorry for him—he'd confess to being Ethan Blair.

WHEN ZOË STEPPED OUT of the bathroom, it was the scent that hit her first. Garlic and something else. If she'd had any experience with food preparation, she probably could have named the other smells that were wafting toward her. All she knew was that they were wonderful.

Jed stood behind the island in the kitchen with his back to her. He wore a T-shirt and a pair of jeans that looked a bit big and rode low on his hips, and he was chopping things and tossing them into a pan.

Her mouth began to water. For the food, she tried to tell herself. But that wasn't entirely true. She had an equal hunger for the man. And that was ridiculous. They'd just made love twice. Once on the island counter. She only had to glance at it for her blood to heat. The second time had been on the floor. If she went to him now and put her arms around him, he'd make love to her again. She knew it.

Never had she elicited this kind of attraction in a man. Never had she had this kind of power. A thrill moved through her at the memories of what they'd done to each other, for each other. She should probably feel guilty for the time she'd spent with Ethan, but she didn't. And she didn't want to analyze that. She certainly didn't regret it. Thanks to the two men, she'd changed.

"I hope you're hungry," Jed said without turning around.

"I'm starved." She was, Zoë decided, and not just for food or even Jed Calhoun. She was hungry for life, for all the experiences she'd been avoiding because of her fears and hang-ups.

When she and Jed each moved back into their separate lives, she would have at least that, along with the memories of what they'd shared. She tried to ignore the little pain that seemed to tighten around her heart at the thought.

"I hope you like omelets."

"I do." She moved toward the kitchen area. What he was making looked a great deal more complicated than an omelet.

He sent a glance over his shoulder. "I could use some help with the toast. And you'd better make the coffee. Ryder says I'm lousy at it."

"Sure. Toast and coffee are my specialties." She

hurried around the counter and plucked two pieces of toast out of the toaster, adding them to the pile he'd already started. Then she studied the coffeemaker. "I'm best at making instant."

"A woman after my own heart. It's fast and foolproof."

The automatic drip pot looked pretty simple. Zoë read the directions on the bag of coffee Jed had set out, scooped grounds and poured water into the appropriate compartments, and then crossed her fingers and pressed the start button. Next to her, Jed cracked eggs and whipped them into a froth. She discovered there was an intimacy to working in the small space with him.

"Do you cook?" he asked when the eggs were in the pan and he was carefully pulling them back from the edge.

"No. My parents had a housekeeper who did the cooking. They felt that every single moment of one's time should be devoted to more intellectual pursuits. Since I've been on my own, I either eat at work or buy takeout."

He glanced at her horrified. "You don't actually eat the stuff they dish up to the students at Georgetown?"

She shrugged. "It's convenient."

"It's horrible. I bought a hot plate and started cooking in college for self-preservation." He sent her a grin. "Most of my dishes can be made in one pan as a result."

She studied him for a moment. "We don't really know a lot about each other, do we?"

He met her eyes. "We know a lot about each other. We're just a little short on the background stuff. And I assume you know at least some of that. You ran a check on me, didn't you?"

"Yes." She could feel heat staining her cheeks.

He sent her a smile. "Good. I'd feel bad if you hadn't at least been interested enough to do that. I did the same thing to you right after we first met in this apartment."

"Really?" A little thrill moved through her that he would be that curious. She'd never forgotten their first meeting. They'd been working on a case involving the disappearance of a reporter for the *Washington Post*— a case that had put Sierra's life in danger. And she'd felt a connection with Jed the moment she'd literally bumped into him at the front door.

Jed flipped the omelet over and lowered the flame. When he turned to her, his expression was serious. "I was attracted to you right from the first. I didn't much like the idea of that."

"I hated it," Zoë said.

His smile was rueful. "Yeah. I got that. And I got a real kick out of annoying you. But when I discovered that I was becoming more and more attracted to you, and I began to fantasize about having you, it wasn't so funny. So, I checked you out. Knowledge is power, and you were taking away some of mine."

She simply stared at him for a moment. "I suppose I felt the same way."

He nodded. "Good." Then he smiled that slow smile that sent warmth through her right down to her toes. "So we at least know the basics about each other."

"Not entirely. When I checked you out, there were a lot of files I couldn't get into. I didn't have the clearance."

It shouldn't have surprised him that she'd dug deep enough to discover the blocks. "Some of the work I've done for the government is classified. I didn't even use my own name."

Her eyes widened. "You were some kind of a secret agent?"

"That sounds a bit glamorous for the kind of work I did."

"The envelope—it has something to do with an assignment you're on. You don't have to tell me—you probably can't. I hope it's not a matter of life and death."

"I wish I could tell you."

"No. Really, there's no need, considering the nature of our relationship." Then noticing that the coffee was ready, she located mugs and filled them. By the time she had the coffee and the toast on the island, Jed was already seated. He didn't speak again until they were seated and she'd taken her first bite of the eggs.

"Well?" he asked.

The flavors were already filling her mouth. She barely swallowed before she cut off another bite. "It's wonderful. I didn't know eggs could taste this good."

He pointed a fork at her. "They don't if you eat them at a college or the kind of restaurant where they've been under a heat lamp for hours." He lifted his mug. "Coffee's good."

For a few moments they ate in silence. It was only

when their plates had been cleaned that Jed said, "We need to talk, Zoë."

"Are you going to tell me what was in the envelope?"

"No. It's about us."

14

ZOË SET DOWN HER FORK. "If this is where you tell me that you can't see me again, you don't have to. I understand."

Annoyance and something else swept through Jed. Fear? No, that was nonsense. He had been going to tell her that they wouldn't be able to see each other—at least until he cleared his name. But there was something in her eyes and there'd been something in her tone earlier when she'd mentioned their relationship that told him she'd decided whatever they'd shared was only temporary.

Did that mean she liked Ethan better? Or had she merely used him for sex, used Ethan for sex, and was now prepared to walk away? Was that all he'd meant to her? The thought had temper rolling through him, but he tamped it down.

"Are you dumping me, Zoë?" he asked.

"We started out with an agreement that—" she waved a hand "—that we were going to have a one-time fling."

"But you came here today."

"Yes. To give a message to Ryder. The only reason we ran into each other was by accident."

He couldn't refute that. But some of his temper eased when he realized that she was interpreting the facts in the best way she could. Perhaps it was time to give her more to work with. He reached for her hand. "I do want to see you again, but my life's complicated right now."

"I don't need to know all the details."

When she tried to tug her hand free, he kept it in his. "I want to tell you what's going on for a couple of reasons. For one, I've involved you in this and I've put you in danger."

She stilled then and sat, waiting for him to continue.

"One of the things I do is contract work for the government, sometimes the CIA and sometimes other agencies. I don't even use my own name. That's why you couldn't access some of the files. Six months ago, I was on a special assignment for the CIA in Colombia. I was to deliver a message to an undercover agent who had infiltrated a drug cartel, one of the biggest. It should have been a fairly easy assignment. Only this time something went terribly wrong."

Zoë tightened her grip on his hand, and some of his own tension eased. He went on, not mentioning names but summarizing the events from his arrival in Bogotá, to his delivery of the message, to the explosion that occurred only minutes after he'd left the bar. Then he told her about meeting another agent in an alley, being shot, and waking up in the small hospital. "So," he said, "as far as anyone knows, I'm still dead. And the only way I can come back to life is to find out who really killed that man and clear my name."

Zoë said nothing when he was finished. She merely stared at him. He could tell that her mind was working. A little line had appeared on her forehead. But he didn't know what she was thinking.

For a moment, panic gripped his stomach again. Maybe she didn't believe he'd been framed for Frank's murder. But she deserved to hear the rest. He had to tell her about Ethan, too. "There's something else you should know."

She raised her free hand to stop him. "I think I already know. I know who you really are. You're Lucifer. That's the code name you worked under at the CIA. I've read all your files and all your reports."

It was Jed's turn to stare. But before he could ask her how she'd learned his code name, the elevator doors opened and Ryder stepped into the apartment along with Gage Sinclair and Bailey Montgomery.

"Sorry to interrupt," Ryder said, "but this is the first break we've had, and I wanted you to know about it."

Jed slid off of his stool. The last thing he'd expected was to see the woman who'd shot him and left him for dead striding into Ryder Kane's apartment. Evidently, it was his day for surprises.

ZOË'S HEAD WAS STILL spinning with the realization that Jed Calhoun was Lucifer when she turned to glance at the two people stepping out of the elevator behind Ryder

Kane. The look on Jed's face had alerted her to the fact that he wasn't happy about the interruption.

She recognized Bailey Montgomery. They'd never had any direct contact, but the woman had been her role model when she'd been at the CIA. She didn't know the tall, dark-haired man who walked with a slight limp. Bailey's expression was serious, as was her companion's.

Turning back to Jed, Zoë saw the kind of hard expression that she'd often imagined on Lucifer's face, and she could feel his tension as if it was her own.

Ryder was the only person in the room who was smiling. He held up a hand as he approached the kitchen. "Relax. Sometimes Muhammad doesn't have to go to the mountain. The mountain comes to him. Plus, Ms. Montgomery comes bearing gifts."

"So did the Greeks," Jed said in a cold voice, never taking his gaze off Bailey.

Zoë stared at Jed, becoming more and more aware of the change in him. This wasn't the laid-back man with the lazy sense of humor that she'd known as Jed Calhoun.

"This time the gift is those files we were going to break into her office to get," Ryder said. "She's got those and more."

Jed said nothing.

"I suppose you'd like an apology." Bailey walked forward until she was standing only a few feet away from Jed. The tall man remained at her side.

"For shooting me and leaving me in that alley? When would you like that?"

Tension snapped between the two of them, and Zoë drew in a quick breath as the tall stranger stepped in between Bailey and Jed. Another realization joined the little tornado whirling in her head. Bailey Montgomery was the assassin Jed had told her about. She couldn't help picturing it again in her mind, and the image made her stomach roll.

But he hadn't been killed. He was here and safe. And he was Lucifer, the man she'd had a crush on for months. How many times had she pored over the details surrounding Frank Medici's death—Lucifer's meeting with him in that bar, the suspicious timing of the explosion? The evidence had all pointed to Lucifer being the assassin. But it hadn't made any sense, not once you looked at the man's history. She'd told Hadley Richards that Lucifer couldn't possibly have killed Frank Medici.

She was still trying to get her mind around the knowledge that Lucifer and Jed were the same man, and the spinning in her head was making her dizzy. She had to work to focus on the conversation.

"If she'd wanted you dead, you wouldn't be here," the tall man was saying. "I should have trusted my instincts on that. I trained her."

"Are you saying she bungled it on purpose?" Jed asked.

"I'm saying more than that. She not only didn't kill you, she arranged for you to be taken to that hospital, and she also arranged for the papers to get you out of the country," the man said.

"So she says," Jed commented.

"I'm not proud of what I did," Bailey said. "My only defense was that if I'd refused the job, Hadley Richards would have sent someone else."

"Hadley Richards authorized you to kill me?" Jed asked.

"The director authorized it and Hadley gave me the assignment. *To take you out* was the phrase he used," Bailey said. "You'd killed a valued agent and betrayed your country for money."

"I believe her," the man said.

"I'm inclined to believe her, also," Ryder said. "You should at least listen to her side of the story. Why don't ᴡᴇ sit down, pool our information and see if we can make some sense out of this?" He moved farther into the kitchen. "I'll make a fresh pot of coffee."

"Not quite yet," Bailey said. "I'm not sharing any more information until someone tells me what *she's* doing here." When Bailey turned toward Zoë, so did everyone else in the room.

"Me?" The spinning in Zoë's head had centered right behind her eyes.

"She's a friend of mine," Jed said.

Bailey turned to him. "Did you know that she's the one who wrote the reports that fingered you as Frank Medici's assassin and show how the money that the Vidal drug ring paid for the hit can be traced to a bank in the Caymans in your name?"

"No." The one word was all Zoë could manage.

Bailey patted her bag. "I've got the reports with me.

They've both got your signature, and they're what Hadley Richards used to get the director to sanction my taking Jed out."

Zoë pressed fingers to her temple. "Mr. Richards asked me to run a probability check on Lucifer as Frank Medici's assassin, but my analysis didn't support that theory." She glanced at Jed. "I didn't know you were Lucifer. And I never heard the name Jed Calhoun until we met here in this apartment two weeks ago."

"What about the report on the money? That has your name on it, too," Bailey said.

Zoë frowned. "I didn't write it."

"Liar," Bailey said.

"She's not a liar." Jed moved then, cutting in front of Bailey to take Zoë's arm.

"When she resigned, there were rumors that she was sleeping with Richards," Bailey said. "She could be covering for him now."

Zoë felt Jed's hand tighten on her arm, but she couldn't meet his eyes. The hammering in her head had begun to roar in her ears.

"Ryder, she needs aspirin," Jed said as he led her to the sofa in the living area. Then he turned back to Bailey. "I'd trust Zoë McNamara with my life."

For a moment there was a tense silence in the room. Zoë simply stared at Jed. She couldn't even begin to identify the flood of feelings pouring through her.

It was Ryder who finally spoke. "Well, it's clear we'll have to work through some trust issues here."

"I'll vouch for Bailey," the tall man said.

"I'll vouch for Zoë," Jed said.

"That's good enough for me," Ryder said. "Can we agree for the time being to take the two ladies at their words?"

Zoë met Bailey's eyes and said, "Yes."

"Okay," Bailey agreed.

"Why don't all of you sit down," Ryder suggested. "Everyone can tell his or her side of the story, and maybe together we can figure out what the hell is going on."

FIFTEEN MINUTES LATER, they were all gathered on or near the sofas flanking the large coffee table in the living area of Ryder's apartment. Zoë felt a sense of déjà vu; she'd sat on the same place on the same sofa when she'd first met Jed.

But everything was different now. Jed wasn't sitting directly across from her. Instead, he was pacing back and forth behind one of the sofas. And he wasn't Jed. At least he wasn't the easygoing man with the mocking manner that she'd seen him as that night.

He was Lucifer. And she was having trouble reconciling the two.

She would have to think about that later. Right now, she had to concentrate on the fact that Jed Calhoun was in trouble. He'd been framed for a murder. In spite of her report, Lucifer had been blamed for Frank Medici's death.

Zoë made an effort to focus her attention on the discussion that was going on around her. The tall man sitting at the end of the couch with one leg extended was Gage Sinclair. This had been the man, she'd learned, who'd had the envelope delivered to her at the Blue Pepper so that she could pass it on to Jed.

Ryder had brought a whiteboard into the room and was busily writing down notes as each of them talked. Bailey Montgomery was perched on the arm of the sofa next to Gage, and she was frowning at Ryder's notes.

Jed had told his story first, recapping how he'd been contacted by Agent Montgomery at the CIA and asked to deliver a message to Frank Medici. There was a chance that Frank's cover had been penetrated so urgency was key.

Ryder took him over the same details that she'd spent so much time analyzing—how he'd met Frank at the designated bar and delivered the message. Then seconds after he'd left the bar, the bomb had gone off.

Bailey went next, taking the files out of her bag and placing them on the coffee table. When she'd summarized the contents and Ryder had added pertinent details to the whiteboard, Zoë opened the file with her name on it and studied her signatures.

"They certainly look like mine," she said. "But I never wrote those reports. I ran all the data on Lucifer, and then I added my own analysis. That part's been expunged. I wrote that Lucifer was just not the type of agent to suddenly take drug money and arrange to kill an old colleague. I told Mr. Richards that twice when I handed in the reports."

"How did he react?" Ryder asked.

Zoë clasped her hands tightly together. "After I handed in the first one, he asked me to run the analysis again and told me it was urgent. I was to deliver the results to him at the Four Seasons because he would be spending the night in D.C. After the second run-through, my analysis didn't change."

"What about the report that showed the money in an account Jed had taken out in the Caymans?" Bailey asked.

"I didn't write that one. Mr. Richards and I…had a problem. He asked for my resignation a few days after I submitted my second analysis on Lucifer."

"What kind of problem?" Jed asked.

Zoë lifted her chin. She knew what he was asking, and heat flooded her cheeks. He wanted to know about Bailey's accusation. "The problem isn't relevant. The important thing is that someone forged my name to those reports."

"Something that would probably never have come to light after you'd resigned." Bailey studied Zoë thoughtfully for a minute. "That wasn't the first time that Hadley had asked you to work late and take reports to him at the Four Seasons, was it, Zoë?"

"No. He'd given me several assignments to do for him because he said that he liked my work. He asked me on three occasions to join him for lunch at the Four Seasons and make my reports, but that was the first time that he invited me to come in the evening. We had a drink in the bar, and someone stopped by the table. Mr.

Richards seemed upset. When I asked him why, he explained that the woman was a particular friend of his wife and he was sure she would misinterpret our relationship. The next day at work, I heard the rumors that Mr. Richards and I were having an affair."

"I heard them, too," Bailey said.

"And you believed them," Zoë said. "Everyone did."

"Hadley does have a reputation with women," Bailey said. "But you didn't have an affair with him, did you, Zoë?"

Zoë laced her fingers together and stared down at her hands. "No. But two days later, Mr. Richards called me into his office and asked me to resign before the rumors grew. He claimed that his wife would be devastated, and that if there was any hint of scandal, it would be bound to reflect poorly on the administration because of his father-in-law's position as the president's security advisor."

Bailey's brows shot up. "So he played the do-it-for-your-country card?"

"I…didn't think of it that way. I just figured that I shouldn't have been so naive. Looking back, I can see that meeting him that way outside of the office in a public place, it could appear that we were having an affair," Zoë said.

"He was your boss. You met with him at his request," Jed pointed out.

Zoë glanced at him, but she couldn't read what he was thinking.

"Yes, but I could have refused. I should have. And

when he asked me to resign, he apologized, claiming that it was all his fault. He'd so admired my work that he'd allowed himself to forget how much appearances counted in D.C."

Ryder added notes to the whiteboard. "So Zoë's a newbie at the agency. She writes the analysis on Lucifer and she leaves at Hadley Richards's request."

"So if there are questions later about the reports, she's not around to contradict what they say," Jed added.

"Neat," Gage murmured. "Very neat."

"I agree," Ryder said, "Zoë is out of the way and the reports are in, damning Lucifer for the murder of Frank Medici. There's an order from the director to take out Lucifer." He tapped the board with the marker thoughtfully. "The man with his finger in every pie seems to be Hadley Richards."

"The question is why?" Bailey said.

For a few minutes, there was silence in the room as everyone stared at the whiteboard.

Bailey looked at Jed and spoke again. "I was hoping that if and when you resurfaced, you might have an idea of why you were framed. Do you have some sort of history with Hadley Richards that would threaten him?"

Jed shook his head. "I've never even met him."

"He's out to get the director's job, and it could open up this year," Bailey continued. "Do you have any aspirations in that direction?"

Jed's laugh was dry. "No way."

Zoë cleared her throat. "Lucifer isn't politically correct enough for that kind of a job."

Everyone turned to stare at her.

"It was part of my analysis." She shot a quick look at Jed before she continued. "He wouldn't play political games. He's too much of an idealist. Plus, he's known for sometimes making risky decisions and skating pretty close to the edge of the law. That's what makes him such a great field agent. I mean, think about 007. Can you ever see James Bond taking over M's job?"

"Good point," Ryder said with a grin. "Bond always needs M to rein him in."

"She's right." Bailey rose and moved to study the whiteboard. "So that means Frank Medici was definitely the prime target." She fisted her hands on her hips. "Why take out the only man who's successfully penetrated the Vidal organization? And why use Lucifer to set it up? Why frame him?"

There was another stretch of silence.

Then suddenly Zoë said, "I think I can answer the second question. Lucifer is the perfect choice. Frank trusted him because they have a history together." She paused to glance at Gage and Ryder. "Both of you would have trusted him, right?"

Ryder and Gage made sounds of agreement.

"And who would be the person most likely to start poking into the circumstances surrounding Frank's death?" Zoë asked.

"Lucifer," Bailey said. "And the bomb didn't take care of that problem."

"No. I was close to finding out who'd made that bomb when you asked me to meet with you in that alley," Jed added. "So if we're right, that's why I had to be eliminated."

"If Richards is behind all this, he came up with a brilliant master plan," Gage said. "First he has Bailey contact Lucifer to contact Frank. Then once Frank is dead and Lucifer is properly framed, he assigns her the job of taking Lucifer out. Not only does he eliminate Lucifer, but he ensures Bailey's loyalty. She's not likely to start poking around in it because she's involved right up to her pretty little neck."

Jed picked up the thread. "He takes Zoë under his wing, assigns her the reports, and when she sticks by her analysis, he orchestrates her resignation so that he can doctor her reports."

"In a matter of days, the frame's in place, both Lucifer and Frank Medici are dead, and the cases are closed," Ryder summarized. "I have to agree with Gage. It's a brilliant master plan."

Bailey shot Zoë a grim smile. "It might even have worked if old Had hadn't underestimated the women he chose as his pawns."

"Very true," Gage said with a smile for both women.

"But we still don't know why Richards wanted Frank Medici dead," Jed pointed out.

"Frank didn't even work under Hadley," Bailey

said. "And I could never find any kind of a link between them."

"Wait a minute." Zoë reached for the reports that Bailey had placed on the coffee table earlier and began scanning the one about the money trail. After skimming it, she glanced up. "The money in Lucifer's account in the Caymans—there's no doubt that it can be traced to the Vidal organization?"

"None," Bailey said.

"Then that's the link," Zoë said. "If Richards is behind all this, he's got a connection to the Vidal drug cartel."

"She's right." Jed rose from the sofa, grabbed her by the shoulders and lifted her up for a smacking kiss. "You're brilliant, and Hadley Richards was a fool to let you resign."

Ryder tapped on the whiteboard again this time to get their attention. "Before we start to celebrate, we have some work ahead of us. Knowing that there is a connection is a far cry from discovering what it is. But since we have some of the CIA's best gathered in this room, we ought to be able to dig up something. Here's the plan."

15

ZOË STUDIED her computer screen. Ryder had assigned
each of them tasks and rooms to work in. He'd taken
Gage and Bailey to his business offices on the floor
below, and she and Jed were using the equipment he
kept in his apartment. Jed had chosen a wireless laptop,
leaving her with the desktop computer. Then, without a
word to her, he'd moved into the living room.

The action only confirmed what she'd already
sensed. He was withdrawing from her just as she'd
expected. Once they cleared his name, he'd go back to
being Lucifer, and she'd never see him again.

She couldn't think about that now. She couldn't allow
the feelings swamping her to distract her. Her job was
to investigate the corporate holdings of McManus Pharmaceuticals, which was the company that Hadley Richards's wife's family owned. Priscilla McManus Richards
was the current CEO. Zoë had volunteered to look at
McManus because there'd been something nibbling at
the back of her mind, the kind of hunch that she sometimes got when she was pursuing a new line of research.

The hunch might pay off if she could just keep

focused. It had taken her over an hour, but she'd managed to access a list of the company's holdings. At first glance, nothing had rung a bell. But she wasn't giving the list her full attention.

No matter how she tried, she couldn't stop her mind from circling back to Jed Calhoun and Lucifer.

Why hadn't she had even a clue that Jed was Lucifer? Shouldn't she have sensed some connection between the agent she'd been so obsessed with and the man she'd felt such an instant and strong attraction to?

Turning, she glanced through the open doorway of Ryder's office. She could see Jed sitting at the kitchen island, his fingers flying over the keys of the laptop. In profile, his face had the warrior look that she'd always imagined when she'd fantasized about Lucifer.

Then she thought of the way Jed had paced like some kind of large caged cat when they'd all been brainstorming a short time before. He'd radiated an air of reckless danger that she'd always imagined Lucifer would have.

Now that she thought about it, even Jed's sense of humor coincided with that dry wit she'd detected in some of Lucifer's reports.

She should have made the connection sooner. There was only one explanation for why she hadn't. She'd let that overwhelming attraction she'd felt for both men blindside her.

The same thing had happened with Ethan Blair, she reminded herself. And if she was going to do a thorough analysis of how blind she could be when it came to men, she'd better add Hadley Richards to the list. She might not have had an affair with him, but she'd been so thrilled with his attention and approval that she'd let him use her.

Why was she so stupid when it came to men? She hadn't seen through Hadley any more than she'd seen beneath the surface of Jed Calhoun. And she'd always prided herself on being intelligent.

A little flame of anger began to burn inside of her. Rising from her chair, she began to pace back and forth in the small office space. She was a doctoral student in psychology for heaven's sake. It was time she did an analysis of the men in her life.

Her father had never loved her. She didn't think either of her parents had. They'd only been interested in their work and in what she could achieve in the academic world that would reflect well on them.

Next on her list was Hadley Richards. Hadley certainly hadn't attracted her in the same primitive way that Jed or Ethan had. He'd been kind, understanding—a substitute father figure. And he'd been the first man in her entire life who'd paid any kind of attention to her. He'd praised her work. He'd offered her jobs that he'd been sure only *she* could do. Her father had never once praised her work. Hadley had taken the time for her, and she'd been completely overcome by the attention.

Poor, pathetic little Zoë. Disgusted, she nearly kicked her chair. But this wasn't about her, she reminded herself. This was about the men.

Hadley had used her. Pausing at the window, she stared through the glass, but it wasn't the view of the Mall that grabbed her attention. She was picturing her first interview in Hadley Richards's office. He'd offered her tea—somehow he'd known that she preferred it. He'd told her he'd heard good things about her. There was a private matter that he'd wanted her to research and to keep completely confidential. No written report, no file. She was to report on it verbally to him.

Again, she experienced a little nibbling at the edge of her mind. Ruthlessly, she pushed it aside. First she was going to finish with Hadley Richards. Had he set her up from day one, sweet-talking her, inviting her to those business lunches, knowing full well that he was going to ask for her resignation and forge her name to reports that had nearly gotten Jed killed?

Of course he had. The piece of slime. She could picture him poring over her résumé, looking at the photo that she'd submitted with it and saying to himself, "Yes, she'll make the perfect patsy!"

And she had. Needy little Zoë had just lapped up all of his attention like a hungry kitten licked cream.

And she'd been ripe for Jed Calhoun's attention, too. Sex starved, that's what she'd been. And he'd probably known it. All that teasing, the mocking looks, the hand on her arm, at her waist. He'd known exactly what effect he'd had on her.

She pulled her hair free of the ponytail and ran her hand through it. He'd known all right. She was the kind of woman who was an open book to a man like Jed Calhoun. Whirling, she moved to the open doorway of the office. He was totally focused on the data he'd brought up on the screen.

The fact that he could concentrate on the assignment, and she couldn't, fanned the flame of anger inside of her even higher. But even as she huffed out a breath, she knew that she wasn't angry at Jed in the same way she was at Hadley.

There was a big difference between the two men. She couldn't accuse Jed of using her. She was the one who'd propositioned him and who'd come to Ryder's office this morning secretly hoping that she would see him, hoping that he would touch her again.

And she was in love with him. The realization slammed into her with the force of a Mack truck. Breathless, head spinning, she gripped the side of the doorjamb and wondered that she could still stand. The panic clawing its way through her nearly made her knees buckle. How could she be in love with Jed Calhoun? She barely knew the man. She hadn't had a clue that he was really Lucifer. What she was feeling right now was just an aftermath of the great sex they'd had. Women—even smart women—confused the two. Frequently.

She pressed a hand against her stomach. That must be it.

Or—better still—she was letting her crush on Lucifer influence her. Yes, that had to be it.

But as she continued to look at Jed, none of the emotions streaming through her dissipated in the wake of cool logic.

Still, she was sure she was right. It had to be the combination of great sex and her fixation on Lucifer that had her heart doing cartwheels. Because if she'd been in love with Jed Calhoun, how could she have run off with Ethan Blair and let him seduce her?

Would her next realization be that she was in love with Ethan Blair, too?

The thought had barely entered her mind when Jed's head whipped around and his eyes met hers.

Later, she would try to analyze just what it was that triggered the realization. Was it their eyes meeting that reminded her of that moment at the Blue Pepper when she'd first locked gazes with Ethan? Was it simply that falling in love made you see things more clearly?

Or maybe it was just the fury that was still rolling around inside of her, trying to find a release valve. Whatever it was, she moved at the same time he did and when they met in the middle of the kitchen, she lifted the sleeve of his T-shirt and saw the bandage. Ripping it free, she found the jagged and still angry-looking mark that the bullet had left.

"You're Ethan Blair." And then she used both hands to give him one hard shove.

JED HADN'T BEEN PREPARED for the shove. That's why he ended up on his rear end on the floor. "I can exp—"

She cut him off by launching herself at him. The next thing he knew, his shoulders were pinned to the floor and she was straddling him. Her fist connected with his jaw before he could prevent it. He tasted blood where his teeth had clamped on his tongue. The yank on his hair told him where her other hand was. He captured both her wrists and rolled.

The struggle was brief, and he took every advantage he could before she finally stopped struggling and lay still beneath him.

"Ouch," he yelled. He'd forgotten that she retained her grip on his hair. "Stop that. I can explain."

"I'm listening," she said through gritted teeth.

Jed looked down at her. He'd never imagined she could get this angry. Her eyes had narrowed to slits, and they'd deepened to the color of dark toffee. He was amazed by her, delighted with her. Each new layer that he discovered only drew him in deeper.

"Well?" she bit out.

Explain, he reminded himself. Explain why he hadn't told her immediately that he was Ethan Blair. Why he'd seduced her as another man.

Why he wanted to seduce her again right now. But he'd promised himself that he'd keep his distance. He'd even convinced himself that this time he'd be able to keep his word. But he wasn't going to be able to, he now realized.

"Okay, I'll explain it for you then," she said.

He could feel the fury radiating through her, from her.

Panic bubbled up in him. He was going to lose her over this. More than that, he deserved to lose her over this.

"You used me. I thought it couldn't be true—but it is. What was I? Just something that you were amusing yourself with while you were figuring out a way to clear your name? Well, you've had your fun. Now leave me alone."

"No." The bubbles of panic had transformed into a steady stream. He wasn't going to leave her alone. He couldn't.

"I thought you were different from Hadley Richards, but you're not. You're just like him."

Fury rose up, slapping him just as hard as her fist had. Releasing her wrists, he grabbed her shoulders and gave her a quick, impatient shake. "I'm not Hadley Richards."

He had to make her understand. "Last night—I never should have returned to the Blue Pepper. I never should have asked you to follow me. I told myself that I came back for the envelope Gage had left with you. But that was a lie. I came back because I wanted to see you again. I'd promised myself that I wouldn't, that I couldn't, until I'd cleared my name. That's why I—Jed—didn't call you. And then when I saw you last night at the Blue Pepper…"

She said nothing, but she wasn't struggling anymore. She was listening. Some of the panic eased. He drew in a deep breath and tried to push down the other emotions flooding him. "Last night at the hotel, I know that I should have told you I was Jed. I convinced myself that

I was protecting you, that it was much better that you didn't know the truth. I—" He broke off and dragged in another breath. "Hell, I can't do this. I can't even explain it to myself. I just know that I had to make love to you again." He gave her another little shake. "I can't be in the same room with you without wanting you. Without wanting this."

He crushed his mouth to hers.

SHE'D WANTED THIS. Even when she'd punched him, she hadn't stopped wanting this heat that threatened to consume her. Pride and anger, even logic, vanished in the tangle of needs and desires that only he could ignite in her. Greed filled her. Threading her fingers through his hair, she held on, wanting more as his mouth raced down her throat, teeth scraping, tongue soothing.

Oh yes, she'd wanted this fever in her blood that only he could ignite. His hands—those hard, lethal hands— tore at the snap of her jeans and dragged them down her legs. And she wanted the hunger—she could taste the flavor of it in his mouth, feel it pump through her veins.

Together, they worked off his T-shirt and pushed down his jeans. When he paused to get the condom out of his wallet, desperation spiked inside of her. Pressing her hands against his chest, she rolled him over, then she straddled him and sheathed him in the condom herself.

"Now." They spoke the word together and moved in unison. His fingers dug into her hips as he lifted her. Her fingers wrapped around him as she guided him in.

Then they were both moving fast as pleasure built with a speed that stole her breath. Her vision grayed until she could see only him—Jed, Ethan, Lucifer. He was all of them and for now, for this moment, he was hers. Glorying in the realization and in the power, she gave herself to him.

Even though she thought she knew what was coming, thought she'd experienced every nuance of pleasure that he could give her, the climax, when it came, slammed into her and threw her higher. She heard his cry as he joined her, and then there was mindless bliss.

WHEN HIS MIND WAS WORKING again and his senses absorbing data, Jed discovered that he was lying on the floor and Zoë was snuggled on top of him. What in hell was he going to say to her now?

"Are you all right?"

"Mmm, hmm."

She didn't sound angry. "I'm sorry." He winced at how inadequate the words sounded.

She raised her head and met his eyes. "I'm sorry, too."

He frowned. "For what? You didn't do anything."

Her eyebrows shot up. "I punched you and I said you were like Hadley Richards."

"Okay. Apology accepted for the Hadley Richards part. But I deserved the punch." He studied her. She hadn't said she'd accepted his apology, but she clearly wasn't angry anymore. Maybe he ought to leave well enough alone.

Going with instinct, he rose to a sitting position and then settled her on his lap. "You pack a mean wallop, but I deserved it for not telling you I was Ethan Blair. Are you going to forgive me?"

"Perhaps," she said. "I kind of liked him."

"You did?" Jed wasn't sure how he felt about that.

When she said nothing and merely nestled her head against his shoulder, Jed found the gesture almost unbearably sweet. For a moment he couldn't speak, couldn't think. Minutes ago, there'd been so much heat, and now, all he felt was a warmth, pure and true, spreading through him.

"I think that punch had Hadley Richards's name on it, and you got caught in the crosshairs of the anger I was feeling for him."

He tightened his arm around her. "He used you."

"Right from the beginning, I think. I'll bet that he hired me with those reports in mind, and then he seduced me."

Jed tried to keep his voice calm as jealousy sliced through him. "I thought you said that you didn't have an affair."

"We didn't, and he didn't literally seduce me. I don't think I'm his type."

Frowning, Jed lifted her chin so that she met his eyes. "What are you saying?"

"He seduced my mind by telling me what great work I was doing, how he trusted me more than any of the other data analysts. And all the time he was setting me up." Her hands fisted in her lap and her voice tightened. "He knew that I wouldn't go for an affair because he was married. But I can see now that he set it up to make it look like we were having an affair—inviting me to business lunches, asking me to deliver that report and meet him in the bar. He even took me to high tea once because he knew that I preferred tea over coffee. He'd done his homework."

Jed ran his hand down her back and up again. "The bastard," Jed murmured. He could see exactly how Hadley had orchestrated it. "It wasn't your fault."

She met his eyes steadily. "Wasn't it? I was gullible and needy for some kind of male approval. He saw that and used it to his advantage. I'm never going to let a man do that to me again."

Whatever Jed would have said dried in his throat when he saw something flash into her eyes. "What?"

"That's it." Scrambling up, she grabbed her clothes and struggled into them. Then she raced for the small office.

By the time he caught up with her, her fingers were racing over the keys.

"There's been something bothering me all day, something I couldn't quite remember. Shortly after I was hired, Hadley told me that the reason he'd hired me was because of my data-gathering skills. He wanted me to do a little off-the-record research for him. He claimed a friend had extensive corporate holdings, and he suspected that one of them was being used for money laundering. He asked me to investigate. There." She paused to point at the screen. "The company was called Manning Imports."

"So?" Jed asked.

"In my confidential report, I told Hadley that Manning Imports was indeed laundering money for the Vidal drug cartel."

This time, Jed said nothing. He could hear the excitement in her voice.

"I might not have even remembered this report if I hadn't gotten so angry just now." She scrolled down a screen and pointed to a name. "Manning Imports is owned by a company that is owned by McManus Pharmaceuticals."

Jed stared at the screen, his mind racing. "He had you find the proof that his wife's company was engaged in money laundering? Why?"

"I was naive, impressionable, and he knew he was going to fire me under circumstances that I would find humiliating. Maybe he wanted to see if the connection could be made?"

Jed nodded. "And if you could make it, then someone else—like Frank Medici—could also find it?"

"Yes. But I think he'd already made his plan to get rid of Frank. And you. What I was able to find probably just cinched it."

"You're a genius, Zoë McNamara." He lifted her out of the chair and whirled her around. "You're an absolute genius."

Then as suddenly as he'd grabbed her, he set her down and frowned at her. "Hadley Richards must be worried as hell about you right now. You're a loose end. And he's already tried to kill you once."

Zoë stared at him. "What do you mean?"

"Those two thugs who grabbed you when you followed me away from the Blue Pepper—I assumed they were working for Bailey and they were after the envelope Gage sent you. But now we know that they weren't working for Bailey. And we know that Hadley Richards doesn't hesitate when it comes to eliminating anyone who poses a threat to him. I'd say you're at the top of his current hit list."

16

"MAYBE IF WE TAKE IT one more time from the top,"
Ryder said as he set down his empty bowl of chili and
moved to his whiteboard. "We should be able to figure
something out."

Zoë glanced around the room. The expressions on the
faces of Gage, Bailey and Jed were not hopeful. From
what she could see, they were experiencing the same
discouragement that she was feeling.

For the past two hours, they'd tried to look at the facts
from every possible angle. Not even the hiatus they'd
taken while they'd eaten Jensen's chili had helped.

Ryder pointed to his whiteboard where he'd drawn
appropriate lines from Hadley to McManus Pharmaceuticals to Manning Imports and to the Vidal drug cartel
in Colombia.

"In a nutshell, one of the subsidiary companies of
McManus is laundering money for a drug cartel. Hadley
Richards either discovers this or knows it and is worried
that someone else might find out. So seven months ago
he hires a new data analyst, takes her under his wing and
gives her a special assignment. When she's able to trace

the money trail in less than a day, he decides to act on a plan that he must already have had in place."

"Oh, he had it in place all right," Bailey said. "He's a very meticulous planner. I've never known him to miss a trick."

Gage took up the summary. "He either knows or suspects that Frank Medici is about to uncover the real business that Manning Imports is involved in, so he assigns Zoë the task of researching Lucifer, and he arranges for Jed to contact Frank Medici on the same night that he has Frank taken out."

"Then he pressures me to resign and forges my name on the reports that frame Lucifer," Zoë finished.

"And he gets the director to authorize my assignment to take out Lucifer," Bailey said.

Jed ran his hands through his hair. "We've got motive, but we still don't have enough proof to get a prosecutor interested. It will be Hadley Richards's word against Zoë's. And McManus Pharmaceuticals will hire the kind of legal team that will stall and try to whitewash everything. They'll all scrape through it."

Zoë folded her hands together in her lap. "If our goal is to clear Lucifer's name, maybe we don't need more than motive. Instead of going to a prosecutor, let's go to Hadley Richards."

Everyone turned to look at her. She cleared her throat. "Everything Hadley has done so far has been motivated by a fear of exposure. He doesn't want even a hint of this coming out."

Bailey nodded in agreement. "She's right. He's killed Frank Medici and attempted to kill both Jed and Zoë in order to keep this information quiet. It isn't just his wife's company he's trying to protect. He's got his eye on the director's job, which should be up for grabs by the end of the year."

"I think we can get Hadley to clear Jed's name if we promise him that we won't reveal anything about the money laundering," Zoë said. "I'll contact him and arrange a meeting. I'll offer my silence about the forged reports, if he'll clear Jed's name. Of course, I'll let him know that all the information is in the hands of a third party who will mail everything to the *Washington Post* if anything happens to Jed or me."

For a moment there was another stretch of silence in the room.

Bailey was the first to speak. "You're suggesting we let him walk right into the directorship in return for Jed's name being cleared?"

Zoë smiled. "Not necessarily. I'm hoping that Hadley will try to find a way around our little deal and trip himself up." She turned to Ryder. "You probably have some kind of recording device I could wear?"

"I do." Ryder grinned at her.

"No," Jed said. "I can't let Zoë do it. It's too dangerous. I'll arrange to meet with him."

"You can't do that," Ryder said. "He'll have you arrested on the spot."

"You wouldn't even make it to lockup," Gage added. "He could claim that you tried to escape."

"I agree," Bailey said. "You can't meet with him."

Three beats of silence followed.

Zoë was careful not to meet Jed's eyes. It was the other people she had to convince. "I'm the best person to meet with Hadley Richards. I won't worry him as much. At this point, he doesn't know I have any connection to Jed Calhoun, and in his opinion, I'm gullible and easily manipulated. So he'll be less likely to think I'm wired." She smiled again. "And he's much more likely to make a mistake that will end his career if he's with someone he thinks he can easily manage."

Once again there was silence, but Zoë noted that the expression on the faces of her colleagues had changed.

"She's right," Bailey said with a smile. "Hadley will feel confident that he can handle her. Pride goeth before a fall."

"It gets a green light from me," Ryder agreed finally. "We'll just have to make certain that Zoë doesn't get hurt."

JED STILL DIDN'T LIKE the plan. Zoë had been right about Hadley agreeing to meet with her. He hadn't even put up a fuss about joining up with her at the Lincoln Memorial. Ryder had chosen the site because he could put a lot of agents in the area. From Jed's current vantage point on the smooth steps of the memorial, he could see that Ryder had made a good choice.

At ten in the morning, the place was already thronged with tourists, some pushing strollers and others clicking pictures. Some had gathered in the memorial chamber to get a close-up view of the nineteen-foot-high statue of the sitting Lincoln. Others were sitting on the steps, just resting, as he was.

Except for Zoë, they'd each donned a disguise to blend in with the crowd. He'd changed himself back into Ethan Blair, and then added dark glasses and a Seeing Eye dog that Ryder had provided. Fifteen feet to his right, Gage, wearing sunglasses and a baseball cap, sat in a wheelchair enjoying an ice-cream cone. Behind him was his "nurse," Bailey, in a black wig and what he supposed was casual wear for a nurse, snapping pictures of the memorial's facade. The camera boasted a telescopic lens. Ryder was serving drinks at a beverage cart to Jed's right.

Everyone but Zoë was armed. And she was sitting on a bench directly in front of him, scanning the steps.

So far there'd been no sign of Hadley Richards.

They'd hammered out the details well into the night, but Jed knew from years of experience that something could always go wrong. And something usually did.

He couldn't let anything happen to Zoë. Just looking at her brought on the same mix of panic and restlessness that he'd been feeling since…the first time he'd met her? Could Ryder be right? Was this what love felt like?

He barely had time to consider the questions or try to analyze the feeling of joy that had blossomed inside of him when Bailey's voice sounded in his earpiece. "Our quarry has just started down the steps."

IGNORING THE NERVES jittering in her stomach, Zoë kept her gaze on the steps leading down from the Lincoln Memorial. Hadley Richards would be here at any moment.

At ten o'clock, there was a faint breeze blowing, but it did little to alleviate the sticky, moist heat so characteristic of September in D.C. Already perspiration sheened her skin and she took a minute to wipe her palms on her jeans.

It helped that she wasn't here alone. As they'd worked into the night to square away all the details, she'd been made to feel very much a part of a team. The camaraderie, the teasing, the approval—those were new experiences for her. Thanks to the sheltered way she'd been raised, she'd never had much chance to develop easy relationships with others.

If she'd been more outgoing and made more friends during her brief stay at the CIA, would she have been such a ripe target for Hadley Richards? She would never know the answer to that question, but she intended to use Hadley's opinion of her against him.

She glanced over to where Jed, or rather Ethan, sat, his hand resting gently on the dog beside him. Just seeing him settled some of her nerves. She was almost getting used to the fact that he was Jed, Ethan and Lucifer. What she wasn't getting used to was the knowledge that she was in love with all of him.

And he would walk out of her life soon. Unless she stopped him.

A week ago she'd been a mouse hiding away in her

office buried in a pile of sex research, and her only lover had been a fantasy that she'd created in her notebooks. Now, she was actually having real sex—great sex. And she was playing a central role in a sting operation that was going to bring down her old boss. This was exactly the kind of work she'd dreamed of doing when she went to work for the CIA.

Zoë glanced around at the people who were depending on her. They believed in her. And so did she. If Jed Calhoun-Ethan Blair-Lucifer tried to get away from her, she'd just track him down.

Bailey's voice sounded in her ear. "Our quarry has just started down the steps."

Rising, Zoë scanned the stairs. It took her a moment to pick Hadley Richards out of the group of people because he wasn't in a three-piece suit. Instead, he wore khaki shorts and a tan golf shirt.

Straightening her shoulders, Zoë strode forward.

GAGE ROLLED the remainder of his soggy cone up in his napkin and pitched it toward a nearby trash can. "Three points," he said when it fell in.

"Don't you have any nerves at all?" Bailey asked. "There are at least a dozen ways that this could go wrong."

"Which is why it's important to control the nerves," Gage pointed out. "Besides, I'm enjoying myself. It isn't every day that I get a sexy nurse to answer to my beck and call."

Though she kept her gaze on her quarry, Bailey's

eyebrows shot up. "Sexy, I'll take. But I'm not at your beck and call."

Gage sighed. "A man has to have some fantasy life, especially when confined to a wheelchair."

Bailey remembered that Gage had been confined to a wheelchair for almost a year after being shot and losing his leg. One of the bullets had lodged close to his spine, and after removing it, the doctors had made no promises. It must have been pure torture for a man who'd lived the kind of life Gage Sinclair had.

As if he'd read her mind, Gage said, "I thought of you a lot in that year I spent in the hospital."

Thought of her? Bailey glanced down to find that he'd tipped up his head and was looking at her. What she saw in his eyes broke her concentration for a minute. Was he actually hitting on her in the middle of an operation? This was definitely not the man she'd looked up to as her mentor. This was—

With a mental jerk, she tore her gaze away from his and looked back into her camera just in time to see Zoë reach the steps. Zoë stopped and waited for Hadley to descend. Good girl, Bailey thought. That had been the plan. If at all possible, Zoë was to get Hadley Richards to join her at the foot of the steps. Things could get complicated if he took her up into the memorial chamber.

Just then, a youngish man in a lightweight jacket with an iPod in his ear joined Zoë at the foot of the stairs. He seemed to be urging her up the steps toward Hadley.

"Uh-oh," Bailey murmured into her mike. "I'll bet he's got a gun concealed in that jacket."

"Yeah," Jed said. "It's in his left hand."

Shifting the camera slightly, Bailey saw Jed rise and start up the stairs.

"Let her handle it," Bailey said. But even as she spoke, she made an instant decision. "Get someone else to be at your beck and call, Sinclair. I'm going to get closer."

"MOVE." The word was barely audible, but Zoë felt the press of hard steel against her side. Fear shot through her as the young, hard-eyed man to her left led her toward Hadley. Jed was ten steps ahead of her, so she saw him rise and start to climb, the dog leading the way. Out of the corner of her eye, she caught a glimpse of Bailey taking pictures on a step parallel to hers. She wasn't alone, she reminded herself.

"Zoë." Hadley smiled as she reached him. "It's so good to see you again."

She met his eyes steadily. There was a coldness there that she hadn't seen six months ago. She gave him the shy smile he was used to. "I...I don't understand the gun. I just want to talk about those reports."

Hadley scanned the crowd. "Yes, I want that, too. But not here. It's too crowded, and the humidity is oppressive today."

He returned his gaze to hers and smiled, but his eyes remained cold. "If you're thinking of screaming or making a run for it, my friend Digs here has a silencer on his gun. He'll pull the trigger, and I will call for help and then fade into the crowd."

He would, she realized. Considering the clothes he was wearing, Hadley would figure that the description offered by any potential eyewitnesses would fit any number of tourists who were visiting the memorial. And, of course, he didn't know he had four witnesses who could identify him. As far as he knew, he had nothing to lose by having Zoë shot.

"My limo is close by. It will be much cooler inside. Come. We'll take a little ride and chat."

Already they were moving quickly down the steps. A cold sliver of fear moved up Zoë's spine. Jed and Bailey were behind them now. Gage was in his wheelchair and Ryder at the vending cart. None of them could help her without letting Hadley know that he was being watched. If Ryder and Gage moved now, their whole plan would have been in vain.

It was up to her.

They reached the bottom of the steps. Another arrow of fear skittered through her. Then they were past Ryder.

What would the old Zoë do? she wondered. But there was no help there. She'd just let herself be hustled into a limo.

And Hadley Richards was depending on that.

No. The sudden flare of anger spiking through her pushed the fear and the paralysis away. Zoë dug in her heels and jerked Digs to a stop. "I'm not going to get in your limo."

Hadley turned to face her and spoke in a low tone. "You'll do what I tell you unless you want Digs to use that gun on someone else."

She tore her arm free of Digs's hold and spoke in a tone loud enough for passersby to hear. "I don't think so, Mr. Richards."

Several people glanced their way.

Zoë lowered her voice. "Want to bet that someone won't remember your name if your pal starts firing into the crowd. Or I could just scream right now."

The look he gave her held frustration and pure hatred. Zoë had an idea that she was seeing the real Hadley Richards for the first time.

"We can't talk here," he finally bit out.

Trying to hide the fact that her heart was about to beat its way out of her chest, Zoë glanced around. "How about that park bench over there?" Without waiting, she headed toward it. At any moment, she thought, a bullet was going to enter a vital organ.

"WELL," BAILEY SAID. "She avoided the ride to oblivion in the limo. I'm beginning to like her style."

"Yeah," Jed commented. He liked it, too, but it had been a close call. That goon had had a gun pointed at her, and there was a good chance that none of them could have gotten to her in time if Hadley had decided he wouldn't tolerate any lack of cooperation.

"I know what you're thinking, Jed," Ryder said. "But relax and let her handle it. She's smart. Calling out his name put a damper on his plan to whisk her away. It'll take him a bit to come up with a new one."

Jed tried to hold on to that as he watched Hadley take a seat next to Zoë on a bench half a football field away. He steered the dog around and started moving along the path in their direction.

THE MOMENT THAT HADLEY sat down next to her, Zoë shifted so that she could look directly at him. Digs had moved behind the bench, and she didn't want to think about the gun that was even now pointed at her. She'd dodged a bullet so far, but she didn't kid herself. Digs could shoot her, and both he and Hadley could easily slip away into the crowd.

Hadley wasn't looking at her. He was scanning the crowd. Bailey had said that he was a good planner. He was probably coming up with a new course of action right now, so she had to distract him.

"I know that you had Frank Medici killed," she said.

"What?" He turned to her then, and she saw that she had his full attention.

"You had Frank Medici killed and you framed Lucifer for it. You had me write that report on him, and then you changed my findings. I also know that McManus Pharmaceuticals has a subsidiary holding—Manning Imports—that is laundering money for the Vidal drug cartel. You had me give that report to you verbally. Remember?"

"WHAT IN THE HELL is she doing?" Jed asked. "He's going to shoot her dead right here in front of the Lincoln Memorial."

"She's shocking the pants off of him," Bailey said, amusement and admiration clear in her voice. "It's a brilliant tactic. It's going to keep him off balance."

"I don't like the sound of that," Jed said. He was already urging the dog closer to the bench. Cursing silently, he reminded himself that a blind man could hardly break into a run.

"Bailey's right," Ryder said. "She's got him going. Give her a chance."

Jed didn't see that he had any choice.

ZOË HAD HADLEY RICHARDS'S full attention now.

And any minute, the bullet would come. She was certain of that. It gave her the courage to be reckless. "I have copies of my original reports, including the one on Manning Imports, and the ones on Lucifer that you doctored and forged my name to."

"You stupid bitch."

When the volume of his voice had a couple of heads turning, Hadley spoke more quietly. "It would be my word against yours. Do you think anyone would believe you? They'll just think you're a woman scorned who's trying to get revenge."

"Yes, but I'm thinking that you don't want the scandal. And just in case Digs has an itchy trigger finger, I've given copies of the reports to my attorney, and he will send them to your director if anything happens to me."

Hadley grabbed her then and gave her a shake. "You bitch. You're just like her. You women are all alike."

SHE'D PUSHED HIM TOO FAR. The certainty of that had fear sprinting through Jed as he urged the dog forward. Why hadn't she stuck to the plan and pretended to be the gullible woman that Hadley had first used?

As he moved slowly, too slowly, toward the bench, he heard the voices in his ear.

"I'm back," Bailey said.

"Knew you would be," Gage said. "I'm irresistible. What's the plan?"

"We're going to get as close to Zoë as we can. I like her strategy, but if Hadley realizes that he's going to lose everything…"

"Got it," Gage said.

Jed got it, too. He'd realized the danger of her strategy from the moment she'd marched off toward the park bench. As soon as he had her safe, he was going to strangle her.

He was going as quickly as he reasonably could. But the fear tearing through his gut told him that he wasn't going to get there in time.

"YOU WILL NOT RUIN ME," Hadley said. "Do you understand that? I've worked too hard. I've come too far to allow that. Tell me what you want."

There was such hatred in his eyes that Zoë wasn't sure how much longer she could keep on talking. Fear had become a live entity, filling her, possessing her. But she hadn't gotten enough for Ryder's tape yet. "I want five hundred thousand dollars," she improvised, thinking now was not the time to bring up Jed Calhoun's name as had been the original plan.

Hadley shook her hard this time and something dark and ugly came into his eyes. "You're all the same, aren't you? Greedy, lying bitches. She wanted the money, too. In her first year as CEO, she made mistakes that cost the company millions." He shook her again. "That's why she made the deal with the Vidal organization. She thought she knew what she was doing. She always thinks she knows."

"Who?" Zoë asked. But he wasn't listening to her. He wasn't even seeing her.

"You're not going to get away with it. No one will believe you."

Zoë managed a smile. "I'm willing to put that to the test. Are you?"

"I'm not going to allow my wife's family's greed to ruin everything I've ever worked for. And I'm certainly not going to let you."

Zoë felt Digs press the barrel of the gun into her back. She managed to keep her smile in place. "Just give me the money, and I'll go away."

"WE'VE GOT ENOUGH," Ryder said in Jed's ear. "We can move in."

They were going to be too late. That was the fear that had his blood drumming in his head, in his heart. He was still twenty feet away. When he got there, he was definitely going to strangle her, Jed decided. Asking for half a million dollars—that wasn't what she was supposed to say. But then she'd veered from the script from the get-go.

"She's brilliant." It was Bailey's voice he heard in his ear just before all hell broke loose.

Later, Jed would remember everything in a series of freeze-framed flashes. Hadley Richards gripping Zoë's neck and dragging her up and off the bench.

"You won't get away with this. I'll kill you first."

Gage jumping out of the wheelchair, dropping to one knee and taking out Digs.

Zoë using her knee to put Hadley Richards in considerable pain.

And Bailey Montgomery pulling a gun out of her neat little purse and reading Hadley Richards his rights as he lay writhing on the grass in front of the Lincoln Memorial.

It wasn't until much later that he remembered all the details because he couldn't think, couldn't process anything, until he had Zoë in his arms.

"Are you all right?" he asked.

"Did we get him? Can we put him away?" she asked.

"Ryder seems to think so," Jed murmured. Somehow, none of it seemed to matter as long as Zoë was safe. "Who the hell cares if we got him? I've got you."

Then he kissed her.

_17_

"YOU HAVEN'T TOUCHED YOUR WINE."

Zoë blinked and then glanced up to see George frowning at her. Her thoughts had been so far away that she'd nearly forgotten that she was sitting at the bar in the Blue Pepper. The Gibbs sisters were chattering away behind her.

"That's a chardonnay. Maybe you'd like to try a sauvignon blanc. I have a new one, and it's dry."

"No, this is fine." Zoë took a quick sip and found that it was more than fine. The expression on her face must have convinced George of that because his frown disappeared.

The moment George moved down the bar to talk to another customer, she let her thoughts drift back to the same person who'd been stuck in her mind for three days. No. Make that since the day she met him. Jed Calhoun.

Nothing had been right, nothing had been normal in her life since that man had walked into it. In the three days since Hadley Richards had been taken into custody, she hadn't seen Jed even once. She'd filled a whole notebook with her thoughts and feelings about him. A whole notebook in three days! That was a record even for her. And it hadn't worked. She couldn't stop thinking about him.

But he had no business intruding on her thoughts right now. Not while she was supposed to be enjoying a girls' night out. Sierra had come to her office at five o'clock and insisted that she join them at the Blue Pepper.

"Is that wine good?"

Zoë turned to see Bailey Montgomery take the chair next to hers. Gage Sinclair was right behind her.

"It's excellent," Zoë said.

Bailey waved a hand at George and signaled to him that she'd like a glass of the same thing. Then she leaned close to Zoë. "Would you mind telling Mr. Sinclair that he has to leave?"

Zoë sent Gage a startled look.

He grinned at her. "She says it's a girls-only night. No men allowed."

"That's right," Sierra said, leaning around from the stool on the other side of Zoë. She pointed to a table in the corner of the bar where Ryder was seated with the husbands, fiancés, and significant others of her sisters and their friends. "They probably saved a place for you over there."

Gage looked at Bailey. "I much prefer my present company."

"Go," she said.

As Gage walked away, Zoë said, "I think he likes you."

"He's besotted with her," Sierra said.

"It will pass," Bailey assured them. "It always does. I thought he had a thing for me when he first recruited me for the CIA, but it was all in my imagination."

Zoë's heart clutched. Was that what was going to happen to her and Jed? Given her record with men, it was entirely possible that she was feeling more than he was. And despite that it was supposed to be a girls' night out, all of the women who were now gathered in the Blue Pepper's bar had a man seated at the table Gage was headed for. Except for her.

Was Jed even coming? The question had her shifting uncomfortably in her seat. She hadn't seen Jed Calhoun since the scene at the Lincoln Memorial three days ago. He hadn't called her, and there'd been no way for her to contact him. According to Ryder, who'd kept her updated, there'd been enough red tape to require a machete. Jed had pretty much been in meetings with both the CIA and members of Congress 24/7.

There were all kinds of reasons why he couldn't call her. Including the possibility that he didn't want to. After all, he was Lucifer. It was only natural now that his name was cleared that he would return to the life of a superspy.

"Bailey, now that you're here," Sierra said, "we can make a toast. Why don't you do the honors?"

"To Zoë McNamara, one of the best data analysts at the CIA." Bailey leaned close to Zoë. "The director wants you back. He listened to that tape, and he was very impressed. He thinks you have real potential for fieldwork. I'm supposed to talk you into it."

"To Zoë. To Zoë," the other women echoed as they began to clink glasses.

Zoë barely had a chance to absorb what Bailey had said, let alone take a sip of her wine, before Rad nudged his way to her chair and handed her an engraved card.

"For your eyes only," he murmured in a voice only she could hear.

All that appeared on the card were three initials intertwined: *LJE*.

LJE. Even as Zoë frowned down at the letters, her heart began to beat a little faster. After turning the card over, she saw that it was blank. That's all? A card with three initials?

Suddenly, she knew exactly what the initials stood for. Lucifer, Jed and Ethan. Her heart leaped with joy just before the panic bubbled up.

"If you'll follow me," Rad said in a soft voice. "The gentleman is waiting in the private dining room."

"In a minute." The panic was now threatening to explode through her system. She wasn't ready for this.

She could leave. No one would stop her. But she didn't want to leave. Hadn't she decided that the running away part of her life was over? Hadn't she decided that if Jed had it in his mind to walk away from her, she'd just follow him and wear him down?

Zoë set down her wineglass with a little snap and looked at the women gathered around her. "I'll be right back."

NERVES JITTERING, Jed paced back and forth in the small private dining room on the second floor of the Blue Pepper. He'd never had trouble handling a woman, but he couldn't for the life of him think of what he was going to do once Zoë walked through that door.

He'd think of something. He always did. Hadn't he spent his life improvising to get himself out of tight spots?

In the past three days, he'd spoken with the director of the CIA, with more congressmen than he'd ever wanted to meet, and with a crack attorney Gage had hired for him. In the end, it had been the tape of Zoë's conversation with Hadley Richards that had cleared his name.

And he owed it all to Zoë.

But he still didn't know what he was going to say to her. He knew what he wanted, but the words simply hadn't come. He hadn't even been able to write a message on that card. All he could think of was writing the initials. Would she know what they meant?

Every time he thought about her, he replayed those moments in his mind in front of the Lincoln Memorial when Hadley Richards had been so close to her and he'd been so far away. When he thought about what could have happened—

The sound of the door opening had him whirling, and the moment he saw her, words flew out of his reach.

For a moment the silence stretched between them. All Jed could do was watch as she glanced around the room. Rad and George had decorated it for the occasion. Snow-white linen, flowers and gleaming silver graced the tables. Champagne chilled in a bucket and balloons hung from the ceiling.

Zoë frowned. "What is all this?"

He managed a smile. "I'm hoping it's a celebration."

"Oh, yes." She relaxed a bit. "I heard that you've gotten your life back. I'm happy for you."

Happy for him? Jed's heart sank. She sounded as though they were nothing more than polite strangers. Was that what she thought? Was that what she wanted?

"Zoë…" He took two steps toward her before she held up a hand. "What?" he asked.

"You didn't call," she said.

"I—" He'd lost count of the number of times he'd dialed her number and disconnected his cell.

"It's been three days and you didn't call." He took another step toward her, but she held up her hand again. "I'm sorry. I didn't mean to come in here and accuse you of that. I know you must have been busy."

"It wasn't that. There are things I want to say that I couldn't say over the phone."

"Fine. Okay." She drew in a breath and looked as if she were bracing herself. "Go ahead."

But the words were still eluding him. How many times had this tiny woman robbed him of speech? Temper joined the other feelings that were tumbling through him. "No other woman has ever made me tongue-tied," he snapped.

She crossed her arms in front of her and began to tap one foot. "Okay, since you seem to need help finding words, how about I say them for you? You want to thank me for helping you get your life back and regain your reputation. And you're probably having this little celebration to show your gratitude. But it's not necessary. We both know that I'm not the superhero that everyone is making me out to be. All of us worked on the plan to trap Hadley Richards, and it took each one of us to pull it off. I'd be dead now if it weren't for all of you."

"I know." He also knew that she might have been dead anyway.

A beat of silence followed.

Her chin lifted. "As it is, I've got my life back, too. And Bailey just told me that the director would like me to come back to work for the CIA. Gage and Ryder have both offered me jobs if I ever want to leave the academic world. And I think I do. My parents will have a fit, but I think it's high time I lived my own life. Meeting you and meeting Ethan has helped me make that decision."

There was another beat of silence while Jed absorbed what she'd just said. They both had their lives back, and she sounded perfectly fine with that. In fact, she sounded grateful. He didn't want her gratitude.

"And I know what else you're going to say." She moved close enough to poke a finger into his chest. "You're going to say it's been fun, but now it's time to go our separate ways. And that's—"

He cut her off by taking her by the shoulders and giving her a quick, hard shake. "Shut up. Just shut up for a minute. That's not what I want—"

There was a knock at the door and Rad poked his head in. "They're asking—"

"Get out," Jed said, not taking his eyes off of Zoë.

"Right. I'll just wait outside." He closed the door behind him.

Jed dropped his hands to his sides. He was tempted, too tempted, to just pull her close and kiss her. He wanted to lose himself in her. If he did, they might never settle this.

"Dammit." He took a step back. "I've never had a problem dealing with a woman before. But with you I'm clueless." Panic gripped his gut and he ruthlessly fought it. "So I'll just say it. I know that we had an agreement when all this started, but that's changed for me. I need to know if it's changed for you."

He watched the little line appear on her forehead.

"Changed how?"

He fisted his hands at his sides. He was aching now with the need to touch her. "Changed completely. That's how. Dammit, I love you, Zoë. I want to be a part of your life. I want you to be a part of mine. I need you to tell me what you want, what you feel." He grabbed her and gave her another little shake. "There. Is that clear enough?"

"I think I need to sit down," she said.

"Fine." He half dragged her to a nearby chair. No sooner had she settled herself than he dug into his pocket and brought out the box. "I got this."

When he opened the box, she stared at the ring and blinked. "You're going to have to shut that. I can't think."

He snapped the box shut. "Fine." Then he grabbed her by the shoulders and hauled her out of the chair. "I'm not taking that as a no. I am not taking a no from you. I know I'm probably rushing things. We can wait with the ring. We'll date. We'll take things slowly. We'll go fishing together—do you like fishing?"

"Okay."

He stared at her. "Okay? You like fishing?"

"I've never fished in my life." She smiled at him then, and it took barely a second for her smile to bubble into a laugh. "You should see your face."

His eyes narrowed instantly. "This is not funny."

She was laughing in earnest now, deep belly laughs that had his anger and panic melting away. He'd forgotten how much he loved the sound of her laugh. He pulled her closer. "Kiss me, Zoë. I've been waiting three days."

"In a minute," she said when she managed to get a breath. "First, I want to tell you how I feel. I mean, it's only fair that I get my turn."

"Okay…right."

"I'm…I'm not even sure who you are. Are you Lucifer, or Jed, or Ethan?"

He tightened his grip on her shoulders. "I'm all three."

"Well, when I was writing those reports for Hadley Richards, you should know that I developed a terrible crush on Lucifer. He's pretty potent fantasy material. Being a man who's into fantasies, you ought to appreciate that."

The green in his eyes intensified. "What kind of fantasies?"

She smiled at him. "I'll have to show you."

But when he drew her closer, she placed a hand on his chest. "I'm not done. You see, then I met Jed. At first, I thought the attraction was purely physical, but then at some point I fell in love with him."

Relief and joy streamed through him. "When did you know?"

"I think just before I punched you in Ryder's apartment."

He tried to kiss her again, but she avoided him at the last minute.

"Then there's Ethan."

"Forget about him," Jed said.

"I don't think I can. But I'm pretty sure that what I felt for him was pure lust."

"Really?" His eyes narrowed.

"He was an incredible lover, and I can't seem to get him out of my mind."

"Well, maybe I'll bring old Ethan back to life someday."

She laughed again and this time she didn't avoid his kiss. In fact, she cooperated fully.

His head was spinning when she finally released him.

She looked a little dazed, too. "Maybe I don't need Ethan after all."

It was Jed's turn to laugh. Holding her close, he rested his forehead against hers.

"One more thing," Zoë said. "I was never going to

let you walk away. I was going to follow you and get in your way until you just gave up."

"Is that a fact?"

She smiled at him. "Yes. And I want to look at that ring again."

"That's two things," Jed said. "But who's counting?" Then he kissed her again.

OUTSIDE THE DOOR, Rad took the glass he was holding against the door away from his ear and beamed a smile at the waiting couples. "I think you'll all have time for another drink in the bar before we join them for the celebration."

"I'm buying," Ryder said as they moved away.

HOTEL
MARCHAND

**Four sisters.
A family legacy.
And someone is out to destroy it.**

A captivating new limited continuity, launching June 2006

The most beautiful hotel in New Orleans,
and someone is out to destroy it. But mystery,
danger and some surprising family revelations
and discoveries won't stop the Marchand sisters
from protecting their birthright…
and finding love along the way.

SPECIAL PRICE!

This riveting new saga begins with

by national bestselling author

JUDITH ARNOLD

The party at Hotel Marchand is in full swing when the lights suddenly go out. What does head of security Mac Jensen do first? He's torn between two jobs—protecting the guests at the hotel and keeping the woman he loves safe.

A woman to protect. A hotel to secure. And no idea who's determined to harm them.

On Sale June 2006

www.eHarlequin.com

HMITD

If you enjoyed what you just read,
then we've got an offer you can't resist!

Take 2 bestselling
love stories FREE!

Plus get a FREE surprise gift!

Clip this page and mail it to Harlequin Reader Service®

IN U.S.A.	IN CANADA
3010 Walden Ave.	P.O. Box 609
P.O. Box 1867	Fort Erie, Ontario
Buffalo, N.Y. 14240-1867	L2A 5X3

YES! Please send me 2 free Harlequin® Blaze™ novels and my free surprise gift. After receiving them, if I don't wish to receive anymore, I can return the shipping statement marked cancel. If I don't cancel, I will receive 6 brand-new novels each month, before they're available in stores! In the U.S.A., bill me at the bargain price of $3.99 plus 25¢ shipping and handling per book and applicable sales tax, if any*. In Canada, bill me at the bargain price of $4.47 plus 25¢ shipping and handling per book and applicable taxes**. That's the complete price and a savings of at least 10% off the cover prices—what a great deal! I understand that accepting the 2 free books and gift places me under no obligation ever to buy any books. I can always return a shipment and cancel at any time. Even if I never buy another book from Harlequin, the 2 free books and gift are mine to keep forever.

151 HDN D7ZZ
351 HDN D72D

Name	(PLEASE PRINT)	
Address	Apt.#	
City	State/Prov.	Zip/Postal Code

Not valid to current Harlequin® Blaze™ subscribers.

Want to try two free books from another series?
Call 1-800-873-8635 or visit www.morefreebooks.com.

* Terms and prices subject to change without notice. Sales tax applicable in N.Y.
** Canadian residents will be charged applicable provincial taxes and GST.
   All orders subject to approval. Offer limited to one per household.
* and ™ are registered trademarks owned and used by the trademark owner and/or its licensee.

BLZ05   ©2005 Harlequin Enterprises Limited.

**Hidden in the secrets of antiquity,
lies the unimagined truth...**

Introducing

a brand-new line filled with mystery
and suspense, action and adventure,
and a fascinating look into history.

And it all begins with DESTINY.

n a sealed crypt in
France, where the
terrifying legend of
the beast of Gevaudan
begins to unravel,
Annja Creed discovers
a stunning artifact
that will seal her destiny.

*Available every other
month starting
July 2006, wherever
you buy books.*

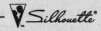

SPECIAL EDITION™

Welcome to Danbury Way— where nothing is as it seems...

Megan Schumacher has managed to maintain a low profile on Danbury Way by keeping the huge success of her graphics business a secret. But when a new client turns out to be a neighbor's sexy ex-husband, rumors of their developing romance quickly start to swirl.

THE RELUCTANT CINDERELLA

by CHRISTINE RIMMER

Available July 2006

Don't miss the first book from the Talk of the Neighborhood miniseries.